ISBN 978-1-332-20680-3
PIBN 10298244

This book is a reproduction of an important historical work. Forgotten Books uses state-of-the-art technology to digitally reconstruct the work, preserving the original format whilst repairing imperfections present in the aged copy. In rare cases, an imperfection in the original, such as a blemish or missing page, may be replicated in our edition. We do, however, repair the vast majority of imperfections successfully; any imperfections that remain are intentionally left to preserve the state of such historical works.

English
Français
Deutsche
Italiano
Español
Português

www.forgottenbooks.com

Mythology Photography **Fiction**
Fishing Christianity **Art** Cooking
Essays Buddhism Freemasonry
Medicine **Biology** Music **Ancient**
Egypt Evolution Carpentry Physics
Dance Geology **Mathematics** Fitness
Shakespeare **Folklore** Yoga Marketing
Confidence Immortality Biographies
Poetry **Psychology** Witchcraft
Electronics Chemistry History **Law**
Accounting **Philosophy** Anthropology
Alchemy Drama Quantum Mechanics
Atheism Sexual Health **Ancient History**
Entrepreneurship Languages Sport
Paleontology Needlework Islam
Metaphysics Investment Archaeology
Parenting Statistics Criminology
Motivational

A TRILOGY
OF DUBROVNIK

IVO VOJNOVICH

PALACE (XIVth — XVth CENTURY)

1921

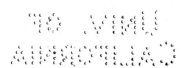

In his Trilogy of Dubrovnik the author has caught the tragical moment of the city's loss of liberty. The three parts apparently disconnected are closely united because of their deep relation to the past. Whatever the characters under the strain of the new life might be doing, the little brass bell in the chapel whether pulled by invisible hands or whether not touched at all, is always sounding, reminding the noblemen of their sacred past.

In "Allons Enfants" where the French army is marching into the city to the triumphant air of the Marseillaise, the poet strikes the keynote to his plays. There has been a great deal of discussion, loud screaming and noise before the fatal moment; there is a great stillness and deathlike resignation meeting the setting sun of liberty. Dubrovnik, the free Republic on the Adriatic, is no more.

The second part of the Trilogy "Afterglow" gives us a picture of the city after its loss of liberty. The problem we meet there is a well known one and somehow forshadows thoughts developed in the third part. "On the Terrace". Here the poet has placed his action in the beginning of the 20th century, we deal with those who have learned to forget and who are seeking to drown their present unhappiness in the deafening din of modern amusements. But there are still those who can neither forget nor understand the new life and we are continually reminded of the past. Yes, in the poet's close relation to the glorious past we must seek his poetical inspiration.

Ivo Vojnovich is a native of Dubrovnik. Belonging to one of the oldest Aristocratic families, he has lived the life he is picturing. I remember him telling me how Madam Mara in Afterglow was a very close portrait of an old friend of his and in the same way most of his characters are traced from life. I am not going to give an account of the poet's life and work here but only say a few words about the subject he is treating in his plays. Ivo Vojnovich, our greatest Croatian poet, has worked out national themes in most of his plays basing them directly on popular poetry. In others again he has developed modern problems, but whatever he does — he always is a supreme artist. I chose the Trilogy of Dubrovnik because its beauty must surely appeal to the foreign reader. Besides it is the most characteristic one of the poet's work, it is so much of him and the past.

During war because of nationalistic ideas expressed in his plays, Count Ivo Vojnovich (then a man of 57) was being dragged around as hostage for three years, cast in prison and treated like a common criminal. In 1917 he was finally transferred to the Zagreb Hospital (Croatia) to cure some severe eye trouble he had attracted in prison. At the present moment he is living in Nice, France.

To make the Trilogy comprehensible to the American reader, I shall add a few explanations.

Dubrovnik, the free Dalmatian Republic for many centuries always knew how to keep its liberty. While the countries on the Mediterranaean were at war, the white neutral flag of Dubrovnik managed to glide skilfully between the hostile parties — trading with both sides. When Turkey grew powerful, Dubrovnik hastened to gain its protection, always diplomatically avoiding the danger of being conquered by the stronger nation. Ruled by aristocrats who were the executive and legislative power (the Senate) of the Republic the citizens (puchani) and peasants (kmeti) had nothing to complain of. There were no taxes to be paid except once a year the people were obliged to buy a measure of salt in the storehouse of the Government. Class distinction was keenly observed, a citizen could never dream of marrying into the house of an aristocrat. What a ridiculous thing it was if it did happen like the case in Afterglow where a nobleman marries the daughter of a merchant. Very often the son of a peasant went out to sea, made money and returned a gentleman, like captain Lujo. No matter what a person accomplished in his life, it was his ancestors who decided upon the place he should hold. The old lady in Allons Enfants reading Metastasio, that oldfashioned rococo poet of unreality, is a very good example of what was understood by gentility. There in the

midst of the new life surging in and demanding a thorough understanding of rough reality, she is deeply absorbed in the placid past,
she belongs to a bygone age. Yes — they all belong to another far
off period, all the noblemen, that is why they are losing the game
and the new, despised generation of common people is going to
fill their places.

Throughout the Trilogy faithfully following the original I kept
most of the Italian phrases mixing into our native language. Of
course, where we changed the Italian word into one of our own,
I had to refrain from imitation. This mixture of languages is
characteristic of the Adriatic shore, a natural result of our close
relations to the Italian neighbors.

Cambridge 1920.

Dr. Ada Broch.

IVO VOJNOVICH

A TRILOGY
OF DUBROVNIK

These three Sprays of laurel-wormwood and heather dedicated

to my Father

during his life, I now place upon his sacred tombstone — — — so they will not fade in the shade of Saint Michael's cypresses.

THE FIRST PART OF THE TRILOGY

ALLONS, ENFANTS!...

ALLONS, ENFANTS! . . .

Characters:

The Duke...................................72 years old
Master[1] Orsat.............................41   „   „
„   Niksha..............................60   „   „
„   Marko 36   „   „
„   Niko................................33   „   „
„   Luksha..............................42   „   „
„   Vlaho 27   „   „
„   Mato.................................70   „   „
„   Gjivo................................60   „   „
„   Gjono 52   „   „
„   Karlo 30   „   „
„   Jero.................................29   „   „
„   Tomo 30   „   „
„   Palo ,...............................34   „   „
„   Sabo.................................60   „   „
„   Luco 58   „   „
„   Antun................................48   „   „
„   Miho 50   „   „
„   Shishko 82   „   „
„   Luko.................................50   „   „
„   Vlagj................................26   „   „

Noblemen of Dubrovnik.

First, second, third apprentice in Orsat's house.

First, second policeman.

Madam[2] Ane Menze-Bobali, Orsat's aunt ....60 years old
„   Desha Palmotica, Ane's granddaughter .27   „   „
both vladike[3] of Dubrovnik.

Kristina, a young peasant girl..................16 years old
Lucia, servant in Orsat's house.................60   „   „
The scene takes place in the house of Orsat the Great, near
Our Lady, May 27th 1806, between 4 and 7·30 in the afternoon.

---

[1] Gospar = Master, corresponding title for a nobleman.
[2] Gospogja = Madam, the title given to any noblewoman whether married or single.
[3] Vladika = an aristocratic woman of a Patrician family in Dubrovnik, the contrary of a citizen (puchanin).

(A room in the house of Orsat the Great. The walls are covered with dark red damask. There is a large white rococo door in the center. Along the walls easy chairs in the style of Louis XIV. (red, white and gold) are lined up; on the left there is a big Louis XIII. writing desk of ebony and ivory and besides it tables of the same style are standing. Upon the little secretary a new empire clock reposing upon alabaster columns is placed. Its face is of black and gold, a golden Napoleonic eagle decorating its top. The pendulum of the clock is a large golden sun disk. Old family pictures are hanging on the walls. Right and left small doors are seen, but not as high and not as elaborately decorated as those in the center. To the left of the stage a big empire table is placed and upon it two or three books and a golden inkstand with a quill for writing. Next to the little table there are two larger Louis XIV. tables of dark Gobelin tapestry. To the right, between the door and the corner there is a large open window. Not far from the little table a golden empire "console" with a marble top is standing. A golden mirror above it, a silver Roman lamp, and two old Greek bronze figures representing the heads of Agrippina and Alexander are decorating its marble top. The floor is of Venetian mosaic, there are no rugs. The parlor is exhaling an atmosphere of cold wealth and order. Its middle doors are closed while those on the right and left are open but concealed by .dark-red silk curtains. The warm May sunshine entering through the window is slowly creeping up from the floor on the little table and upon the walls getting redder and redder. Along with the sunbeams the twittering of the black sea-swallows flutters into the room; They are circling around Our Lady[1] and Saint Vlaho getting ready for their gay nightly hunt. From time to time another kind of noise fills the voiceless room. It is either the echo of people passing under the window or a distant bell upon the Konal, either the cooing of the doves in the crevices of the old palace or the din of conversation, laughter, screaming and yelling rustling somehow subdued and muffled behind the big closed white doors. That room must be covered with damask too, for the invisible animated struggle going on there is concealed so well that it can hardly reach us. But the oldfashioned stillness of

---

[1] Churches.

the house where so to say you might yet hear floating around the
wailing and weeping about its late master Brnjo, the father of Desha
Palmotica and the son in law of Madam Ane Menze-Bobali (you can
almost feel the smell of the incense burnt by the priests who carried
him away) is outsounding even those tiny restless voices; the swallows
are screaming in wild frenzy, and the woman selling salad quietly calls
out into the empty street towards the warm sunset): "Salad[1] women!"
(This natural life of mere sounds and voiceless conversations
among lifeless things lasts as long as it might take you to look over
the whole room and salute the bright sky, spreading and smiling over
the doomed city. Then the big, white doors open parted by an invisible
hand. Like hot steam wistling out of a boiling kettle when its cover
is lifted so as not to spill everything upon the fire, thus at this very
moment a big confused, passionate noise is breaking out from over
boiling mouths and rustling forth through the open gap.)

V o i c e s (breaking, mixing, breaking):
>   In vain! — in vain! Who can believe them? Troppo tardi[2]!
>   Listen to him! — — Ha! ha! ha! It was very easy for Marojica[3]!
>   In vain! Orsate[4]! — — Orsate! che tipi[5]! Anticaglie[6]! Speak!
>   Speak!
>   (Out of this infernal racket an old servant girl comes forth.)

L u c i a (carrying a big silver tray with many glasses, cups, preserves
>   and cookies. It is evident they have just drunk their coffee, but
>   hardly tasted anything. Lucia is dressed peasant fashion but in
>   black; her partly grey hair is braided with black ribbon and under
>   her short dress white stockings and open black slippers are seen.
>   With contracted brows and frownig for fear of breaking something
>   she slowly places the full silver tray upon the little table and sighs).

V o i c e s (sounding louder and louder from the open doors):
>   And who told you! — ah — read! read! Mon Dieu! By no
>   means! — — Why, no! — — — Liberty is the first thing! —
>   A nice kind of liberty with two policemen!

L u c i a (coming again to the doors remains a minute her head bent as
>   if listening, but shaking her old head and softly closing them she
>   returns to the tray wringing her hands in the air. It is not scorn

---

[1] Salad = all kinds of greens.
[2] Too late.
[3] Marojica Kaboga, a nobleman of Dubrovnik who saved and restored the city
after the earthquake (1766).
[4] Orsate = vocativ of Orsat.
[5] What types!
[6] Antiquities.

but I could swear she would say: I wish the Lord stopped their fighting, if she dared. As soon as she closes the door once more the preceding subdued stillness fills the room. Taking up the tray again Lucia trembling what with age what with care goes towards the door on the right. At this minute).

The voice of the salad-woman (below the window):
Salad! women!

Lucia (close to the door, crossly):
May it choke you!
(She goes. Behind the big closed doors in the center one voice is more clearly heard than the others.)

The voice of Orsat: Do you want me to call him?

Voices: No! No! Let him! Let him!
(A pause. A muffled, stifled rustling.)

The voice of Madam Ane (from the room to the left, weak plaintive, and yet somehow void of feeling):
Lucia! — — — Lucia!

Orsat the Great (suddenly opening the big white door as if he wanted to fly out, but again turning quickly to the gap of the black opening with one hand holding the wing of the open doors, with the other one the heavy damask silk drapery covering the entire opening of the invisible room, he is throwing words into its inside, each of them heavy, bitter, burning like the blood rushing faster into his face, like the awful wrath straining all his nerves, contracting his black brows under which his big, grey, unsteady eyes are all aflame. He is dressed like the younger generation of his time. Pure empire. His face entirely. shaved, only side whiskers reaching up half way his face. His hair is greyish. Thick and curly. His big mouth as if cast in brass is lowered in a kind of scornful deep line. The whole appearance of the man reveals restrained ardor, great intellectual power, an ideal exaltation mixed with the hardness of indomitable nobility):
You don't want to, don't you? Naturalo! — — — how could a common man[1], a jacobin — — — a freemason enter into the sancta sanctorum, — — — where are you — — — you?!!
— —. —

---

[1] Common man (puchanin) — citizen, in contrast to kmet (comites), unfree man (Rade Androvich is a common man; Vuko — — — in Part III.a "kmet".

Voices (angered, unsteady, agitated):

You are in your own house! — — — He is mad! Now? at the twenty fourth hour?!¹ No! — — —

Orsat (as before, his head entirely behind the drapery, in a loud voice):

Mad! crazy! imbecile! — — — yes — — — yes — — — that and worse; but when I want — — — I want! (Quickly withdrawing with one motion slamming the doors he closes them. Enthused in the ardor of his thoughts he rushes to the center of the room, but here he shivers and stops. Like rushing forth from darkness into the middle of sunshiny gleam, he stops dazzled, blinded, amazed still trembling from the pain and the struggle he underwent there in the darkness. Orsat shudders and with one unutterable glance of wail and terror he takes in all the quiet fine emptiness. He closes his eyes, then immediately opens them again. Involuntarily smoothing his face with both his hands, he bores his convulsive fingers into his thick, curly hair, Two lines as if carved in iron age his face with a kind of heavy weariness — looking stupidly into vacancy he whispers):

And why all that? (His glance becoming more fixed; unwillingly he steps forward; in a muffled voice full of secrecy): Lazare! — veni foras — — he said and the dead arose. (His nerves relax and a far off shade of a bitter smile flashes across his entranced face; quietly shaking his head and crossing his hands across his breast). He! — — — he was a God. — — — And I? The dead are sleeping and rising, but if the living want to die . . . (Noise and agitation behind the white doors) if they want to? — — —

Madam Ane (a stout little woman dressed in black silk à la Louis XVI., her white hair raised in a "chignon" carrying a costly white handkerchief in her hand, wearing long open-worked gloves out of which her small, thick, white fingers are peeping; she goes straight from left to right. She walks as if going on wheels, neither turning right nor left, Her face is pale, sleepy, motionless. Everything is queer, oldfashioned, I should almost say a little funny, but the breath of the historical greatness of her name, her oldfashioned, very aristocratic movements and habits make an enticing, puzzling picture as if a dusty portrait had stepped out of its frame and grown animated with the real

---

¹ At the last minute.

life of another, unknown period. Reaching the door on the right, she calls out again in the same, mournful distant, insensible voice): Lucia! Lucia!

Orsat (as soon as she enters, still following the current of his tempestuous thoughts, he has unwillingly observed every motion of this unexpected apparation. As if tired he sits down at the little table starting to write something, but always ready to watch Ane).

The voices of Lucia (from the right): Are you calling me, Madam Ane?

Madam Ane (as above, more ill-humoured and harder): Come down!

The voice of Lucia: Here I am! subito!

Madam Ane (returning the same way across the room, dreamy, very old, as if following an invisible procession).

Orsat (rising from the little table holding a letter in his hand again unconsciously gazes upon the black shadow of a woman): Are you looking for something, Ane?

Madam Ane (close to the door on the left without turning around without stopping, without looking at him, in the same inflexible, mournful voice): Nothing (she disappears).

Orsat (still looking after her and when she vanishes bitterly): It had to come to this!

Lucia (coming in quickly but frowning from the right): Here I am! yes! (noticing Orsat) Ah! (she stops talking hurrying along).

Orsat: Why did she call you?

Lucia (quickly glancing at him sideways as if she wanted to say something she did not dare): Why? (grumbling and wanting to go away) Probably for the same reason to-day as yesterday and a day before yesterday (always more quietly, more crossly) and for ever — — — Amen!

O r s a t (looking somehow confused at a letter. His thoughts are already far beyond this room):

What's the matter with her?

L u c i a (as above):

You know master, when she gets something into her head (she has reached the door now, swiftly turns around to her master, looking right into his face). She is wishing for milk from Petrovoselo! — — — — She does not like any more our milk from Konal . . . . .

O r s a t (as above, glancing unconsciously at her):

Why don't you give it to her?

L u c i a (as above, motionless on the threshold drawling a little more in a lower voice):

Why? (looking wrathfully) Tell the Frenchmen not to drink it.

O r s a t (rigid, without moving. Frowning dryly and briefly):

Go! Your mistress is calling you (then swiftly turning to the door on the right he calls in a strong, angry voice); Ivane! Nikola! — — — Pero! where are you? (he returns glowering, excited, full of evil words he does not wish to utter) All — — — All — — — those beasts are running away!

L u c i a (still motionless at the door watching him her head, bent with a speechless almost mournful look):

Master! — — —

O r s a t (sharply, unpleasantly as if noticing her for the first time): ·

What are you doing here?

L u c i a (as above, very low):

I wanted to tell you. — — — You sent them to guard the gates of the city (still more low, almost embarrassed). To-day is · their day . . . . ,

O r s a t (closing his eyes for a minute as if from great weariness he sits down leaning his head upon his hand, then kind of drawling, stupidly, carelessly):

First soothe her, — — — then come!

L u c i a (gently):

I will, master (she goes away).

Orsat (remaining alone in the same place, in the same position, incapable of rising and shaking off all the bitter weakness so suddenly overwhelming him. As in a dream):
Desho! — — — Desho — — — you whom fate is begrudging me! You, too I should call now: help me to lift the cross that has knocked me down on the ground!" — — — no — — — no! — — — even you would not answer . . . . . (bitterly and scornfully, visualizing a new thought that is troubling him) Ah! . . . . . how coarse it is to look at this kind of frightful infamous death — — — the death of old people.

Voices (from the inside getting louder and louder):
What kind of liberty?! ,— — — what kind of independence?! — — — Ha! ha! ha! The mouse and the elephant! Are you saying so? — — —? And I!

Orsat (motionless, the utmost scorn flooding his face; his head bending lower, his eye piercing deeper, his mouth grinning, between his teeth, hissing):
Serpents! "Serpents in the sunshine!" [1] thus! — — — thus! Keep up your fighting!

Lucia (coming in from the left and fixing her sad eyes upon him. She approaches him, simply as if seeing nothing):
Do you want anything, Master?

Orsat (drawing slowly into himself and passing his hands across his face he gets up in all his greatness, quiet, insensible but with a kind of subdued weariness he hands a letter to her):
Go to Rade Androvich and give him this letter.

Lucia (as above):
Do I have to wait?

Orsat (stopping for a moment with an far off glance):
Tell him: "Master Orsat is calling you!" and return immediately.

Lucia (coming nearer and taking the letter, softly):
I will, Master!

Orsat (motionless, fixing his eyes upon hers):
Where, is Madam Desha?

[1] A historical proverb in Italian: Vaso di vipere esposto al sole" !

Lucia (moving away from him and pressing with both her hands the letter to her breast):
She is praying in the Chapel (a pause). Do you want me to call her?

Orsat (simply):
Leave her alone. Go! (Lucia goes without turning around)

Orsat (his hands crossed, deeply absorbed in thoughts):
Whom is she praying for?
(The white doors open suddenly and all the subdued noise bursts forth into the room in incomprehensible sentences, calls and exclamations).

Marko (young, thin, nervous, holding the door calls out excitedly, angrily while behind him two or three tortured, inflamed heads appear):
Orsate, where are you?

Orsat (stands as if cast in marble. Without turning his eyes, without moving his hand. Scornfully as if to himself):
You might kill me now — — — here if I don't't move.

Marko
Miko
Vlaho
(running out of the toom, at the same instant. The doors close behind them. Incensed they all together rush upon Orsat, catch hold of his hands, of his shoulders, in a kind of boisterous excitement face to face as if wanting to melt all their cares into one flame):
What is the matter with you? Where is Androvich? — — — Why did you then send for us? Speak! — — — Move! — — — Go!

Orsat (as above):
And what are those there talking about?

Marko: They are screaming all the time that Napoleon is — — — God!

Niko: And that you are mad!

Orsat (as above, harder and more scornful):
Have they read the letters of Fonton and Sinjavin?[1]

---

[1] Letters from the Russian admirals promising help and asking them to hold out against the French.

V l a h o : Dzivo, the beast is yelling aloud: "Morte ai Cosacchi!"[1]

N i k o : And the Salamankezi[2] nastily said: we are not Greek-Orthodox!"[3]

O r s a t (smiling bitterly):
It is a pity we are not!

L u k s h a (opening the doors. The noise rushes into the room again, he yells out):
The French are here!
O r s a t (trembling all over and rushing towards him catches hold of his shoulders, with both his hands he drags him into the middle of the stage. The doors close):
Beast! Who? Who told you so?

L u k s h a : Just now. Tomo came and brought a pesant[4] who says he has seen the bayonets on the Nunciata!

O r s a t (walking convulsively up and down):
No — — — no, it cannot be!

M a r k o : We are not on time any more!

N i k o : Who is to crush those old noblemen?

V l a h o : And who the common people?

A l l F o u r (around him more piercing, more despairing):
They were trembling before you! Let us lock them up! And we all go to the walls of the city! Let us throw the keys into the Bokar! Quick, quick, — — — Orsate!.....

O r s a t (as if obeying a more powerful voice than theirs, he gets away from them; softly, secretly as if listening to something awful he puts his finger upon his mouth):
Whist! Keep quiet......

A l l F o u r (bewildered, after him in a low tone):
What is the matter with you?

---

[1] Death to the Russians! so these who are against the intervention of Russia are crying.
[2] Salamankezi — the old aristocratic party under the Republic, adhering to the conservative, reactionary ideas of the University of Salamanca.
Sorbonezi — opponents of the above mentioned party, following the liberal doctrine of the Parisian Sorbonne.
[3] Greek-Orthodox (Vlasi) being the religion of Russia.
[4] Peasant — I use this word for "kmet" (unfree man).

O r s a t (looking around him fixing his eyes upon the closed white doors which have grown voiceless, as if they were sepulcheral, he is staring at his comrades, his eyes wide open. Gently, hoarsely, slowly as if in terror):
They have quieted down.

A l l (growing pale and crowding into a clump they are looking frightened at those doors as if the stillness had turned into a human being and they were listening for his steps):
What is that?

M a t o (opening the door wherefrom no sound is escaping): Tall, pale, partly grey, he puts his hand upon his mouth speaking softly and slowly):
The duke sent a message — — — he was coming here now!

O r s a t (convulsively squeezing the hand of his friends looking at them as if seeing them for the first time):
This is death![1]

A l l: Let us go!
(They all swiftly enter through the white doors which close behind them. The noise of the conversation is still heard but quite stifled and very distant. Upon the empire clock the metal, piercing, thin sound is striking five o' clock).

M a d a m A n e (as the clock strikes five, she comes from the left as before, impassive, dreamy, rigid. She goes up to the little table, sits down dropping her hands to her sides, she looks turning her head to the right and to the left as if searching something. She grumbles in a kind of irritated way like a person vexed by many things):
Well! — — — what ails them to-day? — — — there is neither Desha, nor Lucia (looking at the clock) nor Kristina! (like a little child sobbing softly when left alone in the dark) Alas! — — — nobody listens — — — nobody!

K r i s t i n a (red-cheeked as an apple, young as a drop, dressed modestly in a charming white empire gown with tiny blue flakes, a red rose fastened to her belt, she comes in running all out of breath. Everything in her is vibrating with youth, merriment and embarrassment, way up from her black curls and black pupils down to her open sandals out of which are peeping, I should say

---

[1] Death, because the duke was not supposed to leave his palace.

laughing white, transparent stockings. Catching sight of Madam Ane, she stops, putting her hands to her heart):
Alas! — — — Madam Ane! — — —

Madam Ane (whithout turning nor looking, harshly):
Kristina! — — — What time is it?

Kristina (casting a quick glance upon the clock and coming up to the little table quite worried):
Ah! — — — I know: five minutes past five!..... (looking for the books and approaching her somehow importantly and calmy): Ah! — — — if you could see! Madam Ane — — — if you could see what's in the court! — — —

Madam Ane (as above):
Kristina — — — where is the footstool?.

Kristina (bending swiftly she finds the footstool under the little table and places it below the old lady's feet. She remains thus kneeling in front of her and continues animated, gaily, full of laughter revealing this way her overwhite teeth):
Everybody is running! — — — everybody gathering! — — — everybody wanting to reach the gates of the city! — — — Young men with tricolors fastened to their hats! All the ladies at their windows with plumes and .fans!

Madam Ane (somehow embarrassed as if trying to find what was disturbing her):
Kristina! — — — something is smelling here?!

Kristina (she, too is searching for a minute): Something is smelling? — — — What is it? (remembering her rose she takes it out from her bosom. Laughing gaily): Oh — — — it is my rose, Madam Ane! — — —

Madam Ane (hard and void of feeling):
Throw it away, Kristina, it will give me a headache!

Kristina (putting it into her pocket with irrepressible artlessness):
Here it is! — — — let it sleep. Forgive me, Madam Ane! — — — Well, what do you want! — — — The French are coming!

Madam Ane (immovable, like an idol carved in ivory, harshly, pronouncing syllable after syllable):
The French are com — — — ing through?

Kristina (close to her in a childlike anxiety):
And they won't stay?

Madam Ane (as above):
By no means!

Kristina (picking up the thick book, sighing):
What a shame!

Madam Ane (leaning slightly upon the table in a reproving tone):
Kristy, where is Metastasio?

Kristina (quietly, as if her gay flame had gone out, takes the book, opens it carelessly and sits down the other side of the little table):
Here it is, here! — — —

Madam Ane (weary):
Before I fall asleep — — how is that .... (reciting after the old fashion of Dubrovnik, without moving a brow on her face):
Non vi piacque ingiusti Dei
Ch'io nascessi . . . .[1]

Kristina (who knows all of it by heart, holds the open book looking straight ahead and sorrowfully shaking her head, with the right kind of expression):
— — — pastorella
Altra pena or non avrei
Che la cura d'un' agnella.[2]

Madam Ane:⎫
Kristina: ⎬ Che l'affetto d'un pastor![3]
⎭
(A subdued noise is heard from the neighboring room. Kristina lifts her head like a bird on a branch and listening she asks):
Madam Ane!

Madam Ane (as if awakening from a dream):
What is it? .

---

[1] You did not want cruel gods to have me born
[2] a shepherdess; for then I should not have any other trouble but the care of the lambs and the love of the shepherd.
[3] You were born to suffer, my poor heart.

Kristina (pointing to the closed white doors):
 Why are they screaming?

Madam Ane (as above):
 Read Metastasio!

Kristina (quickly turning many leaves she is reading somewhat ill-tempered):
 Nascesti alle pene,
 Mio povero core,
 Amar ti conviene![1]
 (she stops as if something blew into her head):
 Madam Ane!

Madam Ane (startled, surprised):
 Ah!

Kristina (absorbed in her thought, dreamingly):
 Is it true, Madam Ane, that in France peasants can become noblemen?

Madam Ane (almost rising entirely, frightened):
 By no means!

Kristina (sighing):
 And here it is (almost mournfully to herself): — — — Well
 — — — it is all the same since they are only passing through! — — —

Madam Ane (angrily, leaning again upon the table):
 Alas! — — — Kristy! — — — where is Metastasio?

Kristina (shaking her head still more sadly):
 Amar ti conviene
 Chi, tutto rigore,[2]
 (A noise from the room. Inquisitively looking at the door she is listening while reciting the poem by heart.)
 Per farti contento
 Ti vuol infedel!![3]

---

[1] Remark of the Author. Out of Metastasio's melodrama: "Arsace". I knew many old ladies who could recite by heart innumerable rimes of this pleasant rococo poet.
[2] For you must love him who because of great severity
[3] wants me to reach happiness by infidelity. Of Metastasio's melodrama: "Siroe".

(The noise of the people from the street, gay exclamations. Kristina, startled now listens to the noise behind the doors, now to the din coming from the street. She would like to get up but Madam Ane begins to recite like after a dream.)

Vado! — — — Ma dove?

Oh! Dio![1]

K r i s t i n a (frightened, quickly turns a few leaves, and convulsively, swiftly she continues louder and louder):

Resto ... Ma qui — — — che fo?[2] (The noise from the street is getting louder and louder. Madam Ane has fallen asleep. Kristina looks at her and still reciting she gets up and like a finch she jumps to the window.) Dunque morir — — — dovrò![3] (She has reached the window and is looking down into the court.) Ah! — — —

V o i c e s f r o m t h e s t r e e t: Let's go and see them! — — There they are behind the Three Churches! — — No — — no! Along the Posat. — — Move on, Mare! — — Ha! Ha! Young girls! — It seems like the festival of Saint Vlaho!

K r i s t i n a (coming to the center of the stage all boiling with impatience and gaity):

The French are coming — — — and I am here — — — ah!

L u c i a (quickly entering, worried from the right.)

K r i s t i n a (running up to her and embracing her):

Ah! My dear Lucia .... let's go and see the French! — — —

L u c i a (amazed and angry):

I'll give you the Frenchmen! — — Look at her! — — you had better help me to take away Madam Ane . . . .

A v o i c e f r o m t h e s t r e e t: Kristina! — — — quickly home!

K r i s t i n a (flushing with delight):

I am coming, I am coming! — — — (Taking the rose from her pocket she blows into it and fastens it to her belt.) Ah, here it is! — if Napoleon should see me! — — — who knows?! . . . . . Ha! Ha! Ha! — — — (running up to Lucia and ardently

---

[1] I am going — but where — oh Lord!
[2] I am staying — — — and what shall I do then?
[3] Well, I have to die then. (Metastasio's melodrama: "Didone Abbandonata".)

embracing and kissing her): Ah, Lucia mine! — — — here pleasure is coming too. (Looking at sleeping Madam Ane): Poor woman! This is nothing for her (dancing all the time she reaches the door.) Adio, Lucia! — — — Adio! — — — (peeping in through the door, her little head full of laughter and youth). You know! if they stay — — I shall be your duchess! Ha! Ha! (she disappears).

Lucia (remaining speechless before so much gaity wants to make the sign of the cross):
Ah! — — — (almost scornfully and crossly): Oh well! — — — a peasant always is a peasant! (Approaching Madam Ane, she fixes her glance upon her shaking her head): Eh! — — — you would have disappeared a long time ago if we of the people had not been with you! (full of care) but now! I must take her away! she must not see, she must not hear (calling in a low voice), Madam Ane!......

Madam Ane (rising slowly, the same as always but somehow far away, far away):
Has the sun set?

Lucia (assisting her to get up she escorts her to the door on the left):
It will soon, Madam Ane! — — — We might go to your chamber to pray our rosaries.

Two prentices (from Konavle, Orsat's peasants, come in running from the left, all perspiring, flushed, out of breath. They keep their caps on their heads):
The Master? — where is he? Lucia? — — — upon your life! — — — say! — — — quickly!.....

Madam Ane (turning around she looks at them dumbfounded, enraged, great in her mournful frailty):
What manner is that? — — — Ass!.....

Two prentices (stopping and taking off their hats, they are trembling from excitement and fear):
They came to the gates....... the French!....

Lucia (troubled, wishing to take her away):
Let's go, Madam Ane!

M a d a m A n e (as above, looking incessantly and piercingly at the prentices):

Even if they were Turks . . . . this is not the way to come before your Master! (Turning around she leaves with Lucia): Goodness! — eh?! because the French are passing through! (At the door she turns again towards them while they are twisting their caps in their hands, getting humbler and smaller): Well — only this was wanted! (Going out with Lucia to the left. A loud noise is heard behind the white doors.)

F i r s t p r e n t i c e (listening):

They are in there!

S e c o n d p r e n t i c e: And still they are screaming!

F i r s t p r e n t i c e: I am going to tell the Master!

S e c o n d p r e n t i c e: Eh! The worse for them! (They quickly enter the middle doors which slam behind them. A brief pause, then one big exclamation is heard from everybody's mouth, — — — and again great silence.)

L u c i a (coming hastily from the left and taking out a letter from her — — — pocket):

Now I have to give it to him! (She is about to reach the door.)

O r s a t t h e G r e a t (coming out quickly, his face flushed, his eyes flashing. A hard spot is contracting his brows, tying up his forehead. He is dragging along the two prentices, holding on to their shoulders with his hands like claws. Shaking them brutally, he speaks full of misery and agitation):

You! You! — — — and you have seen them! How many are there? Many — — — many, . . are there? All is flashing with bayonets! — — — And the gates? — — — Speak! . . . . . Beast! . . . . Speak! . . .

T w o p r e n t i c e s (in great terror):

They are closed, — — — Master!

O r s a t (waving them and throwing them off from himself like a slough of scales):

They are still so! — — — (The prentices running to the right. Catching sight of Lucia and still full of wrath and fear he comes

up to her grinning as if mocking her, beside himself): And
you? — — — What are you doing here? — — — Why
are you looking at me? — — — I am handsome — am I
not — — — handsome?! . . . . .

Lucia (handing him simply and calmly á letter):
From Rade Androvich!

Orsat (as above, grasping her hand, face to face):
And you, old Lucia you too, are carrying misfortune,
are n't you? . . .

Lucia (as above, looking quietly at him):
He only told me: "I am sorry for your master!"

Orsat (letting go her hand as if all at once peace had entered his
soul. His face clears up, only a kind of hard, great pride is
reflected in every line, in every motion. Quickly, almost smiling):
Who is he to feel sorry for me!? (He opens the letter and
reads it; in an instant his brows contract, but scorn flits across
his pale lips. Calmly folding the letter and showing it to Lucia
with an unutterable expression of sadness and refinement):
If you could read, Lucia, you would understand now what
it means to be a Master! (He stops; bitterly as if to himself):
He is inviting me to a ball the peasants . . . . and some
others are giving to the Frenchmen to-morrow — — —
(He remains lost in thoughts, shaking his head scornfully).

Lucia (involuntarily comes nearer quietly kissing his hand).

Orsat (calmer and calmer, colder and colder, is looking for an
instant at her; then simply):
And she? — — — Is she still praying? . . . . . .

Lucia (shrugging her shoulders and blinking with her eyes):
Well — — — you know her, master! (the middle doors are
slowly opening from the inside.)

Orsat (noticing them, a little startled and calmly to Lucia):
Tell her to come! — — — Go! (Lucia goes casting a long
glance upon Orsat.)
(The white doors open and enter).

The noblemen. (There are some who are old, young, middleaged,
small, stout, in good taste, slovenly attired, but all of them more or
less carry the signs of very old descent and forms of men who had

been masters for centuries, dealing out justice to others. The power
of thousands of years and the innumerable array of irreproachable
aristocratic marriages has impressed them with the mark of a
special though wormeaten, but quite outlined individuality. Some
of them are peculiar in their way of walking, in their motions
and in their attire; some of the old men are still wearing the wig
of Louis XVI.; all the younger ones are dressed after the newest
empire fashion, the way they do their hair and wear side whiskers;
each one an original and type for himself. Especially now when
they are all by themselves when no one of the people or of the
peasants observes or judges them, now when the fatal, historica
moment reveals the secret spots and hidden crevices of their
withered characters and shrivelled souls. Now every movement,
every whisper, every half-vowel has its marked, infallible, true
meaning. A big tempest is shaking the dry leaves of the hoary
republican tree, gradually showing all it its knots, all its rings,
all the cracks of the miserable decayed trunk, revealing all the
nakedness of its burnt, peeled of weather-beaten dry branches.
The skeleton is already grinning under the dried up skin of
rotten age.)
(The noblemen enter talking in an animated but moderate way,
many are holding their hats in their hands or under their waists,
leaning on big canes with golden or ivory globe-shaped handles.
Niko and Marko at once hurry up to Orsat who remains motionless, leaning upon the little table, his hands crossed, scowling
and speechless.)

Niko . }
Marko } (in a low voice, quickly to Orsat):

You know — — — the duke sent a message telling he
knew how he ought to act.

Orsat (as above):
Who would know him!

Gjivo (tall, strong, his shoulders drooping, stout-headed, his eyes
of a sparkling green, his hair grey, dressed in the empire style
he is holding a big cane in his hand. His big scornful mouth,
his staring and impudent look, his flushed reddish complexion
give him the expression of a violent, wild mind. His overwhite
hands are very beautiful. Coming up to Orsat and talking to him
quietly, naturally in a hoarse voice and with a stammering, inter-
rupted accent in a rather confused way looking [at times] sideways at him. He has crossed his hands behind his back):
You see Orsat, I guessed it! They came before we ever

expected them. Well — you understand who has crossed
Saint Bernard and who has walked along — — — hm!

O r s a t (motionless like a marble cast, his voice sharp and cutting
like a sword):
— — — under the Pyramids, Gjivo!

G j i v o (flashing his eyes upon him to see whether he was joking,
then quietly but somehow in a trembling voice):
Yes — — — precisely under the Pyramids — — — mi
capite?[1] — he can do everything. (Changing his voice, somewhat
deeper, friendlier, almost goodnatured): Don't let us be fooled,
now everything is in vain and too late. (There is a noise
heard from the group near Orsat, Gjivo looks sharply at them,
then still clearer and harder): Everything! — — — I said:
everything! (Continuing in a natural voice): We have been
talking a great deal, screaming and saying all kinds of
things . . . — — —

N i k s h a (sitting at the table with a fine smile):
In our own way, Gjivo (taking out of his pocket an old little
book he begins to read it).

G j i v o (startled, he is warming up to his own words):
In my own way, dear Niksha! (anger overcomes him); for I
am crying, screaming and if you want to spitting . . .

G j o n o (foxy, rather small, with a big nose, wearing gold spectacles,
slowly, disdainfully to Niksha):
He does not lack sincerity . . . . .

G j i v o (almost angry):
— — — What I think — — I blurt out.

L u c o (snuffing tobacco, guant, wooden, his eyes closed as with
inexorable grandezza; almost to himself):
Unfortunately! (quiet laughter in several groups).

G j i v o — — — I don't give a cent for people who keep a
grudge — — mi capite? Ah! (Calmer but his eyes flashing.)
Therefore as it has been decided in the Senate we shall
remain neutral . . . . . .

[1] Do you understand me?

V l a h o (tall, handsome, his hair black, nervous, breaks forth):
Nice kind of neutrality to let the French pass! — — —

G j o n o (with irony):
So they might walk across the Square!

K a r l o (tall, stout, of a classical profile a type of Napoleonic heroes,
quickly):
Marmot promised to go out again — and we believe him!
If it were not so we should all be for Orsat.

To each other.

M a r k o :⎫ Ha! Ha! Ha! He believes
L u k a : ⎬ — the Frenchmen! Whom didn't
N i k o : ⎭ they promise so!

J e r o : ⎫ And if they had not done so!
T o m o : ⎬ We should rather have them
L u k a : ⎭ than the wild Kozaks!

M a r k o :⎫ How much for the keys!
V l a h o : ⎭ — — — Chamberlains!

O r s a t (without turning, as if he were not cast in marble, he contracts
his brows and closes his eyes as if they were hurting him).

G j i v o (enraged, because he could not speak, knocking with his cane
upon the ground in a big voice):
Have you started, ah! We had time enough it seems to
me! Three days discussion in the Senate and all of to-day
here! — (more quickly, almost goodnatured to Orsat) — — —
Dunque[1] and as I said before, mi capite, it is useless to get
excited just because one batallion is passing towards Boka.
(Noise and agitation.) And when they pass . . ,

N i k s h a (looking at him through his spectacles and stopping to read
for a moment, full of malice):
If they pass . . . . . (continues to read.)

G j i v o (overhearing it goes on):
— — — then Orsat we shall speak of all you had been
proposing. (Surprised as Orsat does not move, quite naturally
and friendly.) If we had a little row . . . . . .

---

[1] Well then.

L u k s h a (behind, full of taste as if stepping out of Boucher's pictures, smiling at Gjivo):
For Gjivo this is little! ......

G j i v o: — — — forget, as all of us will. Thus we are! Cosa volete?[1] Everything and of all sorts — — — and — — — mi capite — — — godfathers from Puglia[2] (with a boisterous laughter). He! He! ..... He! .....

M a t o (reserved, dignified, his lips tightly pressed, looking far off biting slowly some kind of sweetmeats he is taking out of a golden box):
Excuse me, dear Gjivo, non vi capisco.[3] (Gjivo lazily walks up to Mato, they talk. Marko, Niko, Vlaho, Gjono all around Orsat discussing lively as if wanting to warm him with their hot breath.)

S a b o (tall, old, with thick brows, dull eyes, his lower lips drooping, of an infinite almost naive vanity in his oldfashioned nobility, he is talking slowly, indifferently to Palo and Tomo):
For sure — — — When the emperor asked me in Vienna in French to go to Napoleon as a cavalier d'onore dell' eccellentissima Republica[4] I said (still more slowly): Excuse me, Sir, one who is born a nobleman like myself cannot accompany one che non è mio pari![5] (Slowly snuffing tobacco.)

T o m o, V l a h o and **M i h o** (amazed as if not believing in so much vanity):
Oh!

A n t u n (miserable, shrunk, shortsighted):
And why do you receive him now, Sabo? (laughter in that group).

S a b o (as above to Antun with great sluggishness):
Firstly — — if somebody has to pass through — — it is better the French than the Greek-Orthodox.

M i h o (fat, simpleminded as if coming from the fields):
And secondly?

---

[1] What do you want?
[2] Godfathers from Puglia, means friends who quarrel incessantly like the godfathers of Puglia who always dispute.
[3] I don't understand you.
[4] A cavalier of honor of the most excellent Republic.
[5] Who is not my equal.

S a b o (stretching his words and turning around as if wanting to leave):
And secondly — — — because it pleased me so (noise, talking, light laughter. Involuntarily Orsat looks at his watch as if waking from a long dream).

O r s a t (almost quiet with a kind of iron energy, only his eyes are crying, flaring, thundering. He feels that, and now and then an inner struggle to overcome their fire is visible. He begins to talk and at once excels everybody):
And you think we understood each other and when the -Senate said: Go, — we should call out: help yourselves!

K a r l o : ⎱ Law is law!
T e r o : ⎰ Thus we were what we were!

A n t u n : ⎫
M i h o : ⎬ Oh! look at him! He has started!
L u k o : ⎭

S h i s h k o (old, much too stout, has been dozing until now at the table, to Luka):
Che seccatore![1]

V l a g j (young, charming, agitated):
And my Made who is waiting for me!

G j i v o (to Orsat almost with irony, keeping back his anger and always leaning upon his big cane):
Naturally! Help yourselves and welcome to us! he! he! he! and thank heaven they don't eat too much!

O r s a t (as above still harder, quicker more melodious):
And all we have been discussing here, and what I told you: the letter from admiral Sinjavin who is sending me a message from Slano: "Don't give in, we are here!" — — —

K a r l o : Ha! ha! they are here!

J e r o ⎫
P a l o ⎬ (laughing): Les cosaques! — — —
T o m o ⎭

---

[1] How tedious he is!

Orsat (striking the table with his fist and scourging them with a
furious·look. Firm as a rock inexorable, he continues as if cutting
with an ax):
— — — and Fonton's message!.....

Gjivo (striking with his fist):
That rogue! (A big noise.)

Orsat (as above, always stronger and bolder):
— — — the Curriers, too, from Sarajevo, from Constantinople, were to help us as at the time of the earthquake......

Niko:
Marko:
Vlaho:
Luksha:
} And they will ..... better a Turk than a Christian!

Orsat: And the letters from the Vladika of Cetinje......

Jero:
Luko:
Gjivo:
Miho:
} Graeca fides! — — —

Miksha: They say too: "There is no faith in the Latin!"

Niko:
Marko:
Vlaho:
} Bravo! bravo! So it is!

Quickly, one following the other one like retorting guns.

Luksha (screaming):
If you had received the Greek-Orthodox[1] you would not
have Lauriston at your gates now!

Orsat (as above):
And all this did not persuade you — — — because he is
here! — — He! — — Napoleon! — — — God! And hearing
his name you thought you saw a tearing river, a raging
whirlwind, a crushing lightening.....

Karlo (swiftly, sharply):
Are we stronger than Venice? — — — Than the Pope?
— — — Ah?

---

[1] An allusion to the break with Russia because of the Greek-Orthodox Church
in the City 1772.

Pero: Or than the Roman emperor?

Tomo: Than Spain, di grazia?

Orsat (more quickly, more passionately):
— — — yes we are, we are, if there is behind us he who opened the trap into which God will precipitate you — — — (A big noise.)

Gjivo (laughing uproariously):
And who is? — — — who is he!

Orsat: — — — he who sent you the message: wait, I am near! — — — He who sent you ships to Rijeka . . . — — —

Gjivo (as above):
And Fonton to the City!

Karlo
Tomo } (in great uproar; laughter, noise): Ha! ha! — — — two old Turkish ships! — — — It is true! — — — true! — — —
Palo

Orsat: — — — yes! yes! — — — and Fonton who has been singing to you in tutti i toni![2] When the emperor[3] will be crushed — — — you will have to deal with us!......

Voices (from all sides):
So it is! Again the same nonsense! Heavens! Orsate, get there! — — — Speak! Let him! Why? (Loud noise and crowding around Orsat.)

Niksha (with a blissful smile pointing out to Miho something in the book he is reading):
And what do you say to this! — — — "Non jam regnare pudebit! Nec color imperii, nec frons erit ulla senatus!" Ah?! Sublime!

Miho: Maybe! — — — But I won't give you one verse of Ovid for the whole of your famous Lukan! — — — Per esempio listen to this (taking out a book from his frock coat he recites slowly to him).

---

[2] In all tunes.
[3] Napoleon.

Third prentice (comes in all perspiring without his cap, out of breath, and almost falls down in front of Orsat):
Ah! Master! — — — Master! — — —

Orsat (with an awful look clutching him as if with tongues with both his hands):
Who are you? What do you want?

Third Prentice (as above):
They have come — — — all together. — — — They have covered Posat, Brsalje. — — — Everything is black with horses, with people, with cannons.....

All: Ah! — — —

Orsat (shaking him by his chest):
And the bridge? — — — The bridge! — — —

Third Prentice: It is still raised, but — — —

Orsat (flashing up, he lets him go and the boy escapes; and like a river of passion breaking through the dikes crushing all connecting links, his word flies along with his idea and soars up to the climax of mortal struggle):
Ah! — — — listen! listen! Between those foreigners, their power and their emperor, and between us — a miserable handful of old Republicans, as free men of old times — there is still one ditch, one abyss! The bridge is still raised! Oh blessed be thy mouth, my people, we can still fasten the fetters to our sacred walls, we can still die all united, all free......

Niko:
Niksha:
Marko:
Vlaho: } Let us! Let us! — — —

Orsat: — — — we can still be alone, — — — ourselves.....

Gjivo (brutally):
Are you going to stop their cannons?! — — —

Karlo (the same):
Are you going to chase out the new liberty knocking at our doors?! — — —

S a b o (the same):
Do you want us to be shot by a cannon?! — — —

N i k o: We want to; we want to! (Close to him, furiously, blow after blow.)

M a r k o: We can hold out for a week — — —

P a l o
M i h o } (crying scornfully): Why not a fortnight? — — Ha! ha!
A n t u n

O r s a t (as above convulsed with excitement):
And more, — — — and more! Until all our hills rise, until the people from Boka, the Montenegrins and the Russians join the dance.

G j i v o (mockingly, aloud):
— — — and until they burn us up and rob us . . . — — —

O r s a t (face to face with utmost cruelty):
And they will, — — and will do well to hang us all to our door knockers if we help the enemy of our liberty! — — — (A big noise. A thick crowd is pressing around Orsat. You might think some accident had occurred.)

L u k o (timid, modest, full of consideration, to Palo):
Does one address Lauriston with: Eccellenza? . . . . . .

P a l o (an overfine Parisian type of a Napoleonic courtier, in a half Frenchified accent):
Non mon cher! . . . . . but Marmont.

V l a g j (to Karlo):
It will be necessary, col tempo[1], to pay him a visit.

P a l o: Oh! vous verrez! — — — They will come themselves! What kind of well-bred people they are!

G j i v o (breaking up the group, all red in his face, striking the ground whit his cane):
Ah! you are requesting to dismiss the Senate, to receive the people . . . . .

---
[1] In time.

All: Ah! — — —

Gjivo: Well, say then — you want a revolution.

Orsat (crossing his hands, has come close up to him, devouring him
with his looks):
And if I should say: "I want", would you forbid me . . . . .

Gjivo (looking at him like a tiger facing a tiger):
I! — just so. I! As long as the duke and Senate are here,
as long as we have decided that the French should be
admitted into the city — as long as we are majority . . . . .

Karlo:
Jero:
Tomo: } Yes! Yes! . . . . .
Palo:
Antun:

Orsat (as above, still nearer, still paler):
And who is: We?!

Gjivo (as above):
We — — — noblemen! Who will crush you, too, if you are
against the decissions of the Republic — — — mi capite!

Niko:
Marko: } What kind of language is this?! — — —
Vlaho:

Luksha (with great rebuke):
But Gjivo! The Republic is dying! — — —

Orsat (with infinite irony, without moving, looking over Gjivo from
head to foot):
And who will tell Gjivo: "Gjivo, you can live!" when Gjivo
wants to die!

Gjivo (hoarsely and furiously):
Orsate!

Orsat (as above):
How could we of royal blood sit in the Senate together
with the Stulls Vodopich and Vlajki — when common people

have nothing but their heads — — — (Noise, exclamations, Orsat continues in the most awful brutality of a judge): And you know why we — — — receive foreign sansculottes and jacobins? Ah?! Because when the Emperor is hungry for land — — — he bribes first the noblemen! — — —

Gjivo
Palo
Tomo   } (as if wanting to throw themselves on him): Oh! This is
Miho   disgraceful — — — this is a lie! — — — you have
Vlagj   gone mad! — mad!

Niko
Marko } (with a scornful, uproarious laughter):
Vlaho   Imperial Eunuchs!

Sabo:
Antun: } Greek-Orthodox! Greek-Orthodox!
Jero:
Luko:

Luksha (to Gjivo and to his crowd in a loud voice):

You are worse than the Dalmatians![1] — — — (A terrible confusion. Mockeries calling names, conversation, jokes all these cross in the smoky air. Suddenly the clock strikes softly but piercingly [six times] six o'clock in the afternoon. Its thin sound drowns the tempest and when the sixth stroke is heard silence comes involontarily a stillness full of vibrations out of which one tremulous breathing is heard. It is only an instant, a flush, and at the door appears like fate a red apparition: The duke.)

All: The duke! — — — (And again silence falls like a big black bird with broken wings floating and expiring upon the black waters.)

The duke (enters dressed in his official red cloak, with a slit on his shoulder under which a red suit a la Louis XV. made of satin and trimmed with brilliant buttons is visible. White stockings. Black shoes. On his head a white alonge wig. His face is entirely shaved. His expression is weary, old, with the signs of the family: his eyes look as if they were sewed up in little bags, his lips hanging down. A big gold-studded cane in his hand. Behind him in semidarkness two red policemen are standing).

---

[1] Historical phrase.

Voices from the street (are penetrating the fatal stillness of this moment):
Quick! — — — quick! — — — They have not come yet! — Let more of them pass! — — — Liberté! Égalité! Fraternité! — — — Mare, move on! (Big laughter on the street. A pause.)

The voices of the noblemen on the stage (low, as if dry leaves were rustling):
Did you see him! — — — Who allowed him! — — — To leave his palace... in this attire! — — — Che scandalo![2] It is evident that everything is over!

The duke (has slowly come to the middle of the hall in slow minced steps paying no attention to the rest who are looking at him with different expressions of amazement and inquisitiveness. He is apparently occupied with a small almost ridiculous matter. His lips are moving and a sort of smile is trembling on his drooping mouth. When he reaches Niksha who has stopped reading and ironically watches him through his eyeglasses, the duke looks at him for an instant, then laughing louder and shaking his head he points to the letter he is holding open in his hand):
Here is a letter of Antun Sorgo from Paris. I found it! He! — — — vale la pena[1] to read it. — Just now! And do you know how it begins? (Softly laughing to himself while a little choked by coughing): Ah! — — — My Mare could not compose herself! — — — Just imagine! (Reading the letter with a large golden "loupe" hanging under his cloak.) Eccellentissimo Signor Principe! My dear Maro! Hasn't the devil got you yet?! — — — (Noise, the duke laughing to himself continues to read.) — — — Then — — — "the Republic is still alive then!" — — — etc. etc. — — — (All in his old way, half laughing, half coughing): Who is that devil of a man! (As if remembering something): Ah! — — — lest I forget — — — (Turning to the various groups): It seems to me I came to tell you what you are to do...

Orsat (would like to stop him, but)

The duke (looking surprised at him coldly and absent-minded, he continues simply and naturally):

---

[1] What a scandal!
[2] It is worthwhile. A fragment of an authentic letter out of the library of the duke of Sorgo Porza.

Lauriston has reached Pila and called across the gates of
the city to Luka: "What is the Signoria answering? —
Will she let us pass through the city?" Luka told him to
wait and came running up to me ... (Noise in the street.)

Voices (are heard):
Let them pass! .... Have they fallen asleep?!

The duke (sniffing tobacco he carefully cleans his white "jabot" and
cloak so not a grain remains. Then he continues coughingly but
still frankly):
Therefore I made up my mind to dress and come to tell you.

Luka (aside to Sabo):
"Veramente[1] he might have stayed at home!

Sabo (slowly and scornfully to Antun):
There is more value to a coat"[2] — — —

Antun (laughingly to Sabo):
Than Tinto and the frontier! Ha! ha! ha!

Orsat (shivering like in a fever of anger):
But you won't — duke — so — now! ......

The duke (as above not understanding him):
But what is coming into your mind? — I could receive him
at the Palace with all of you — — — in gran pompa ...
and Tomo and Karlo will go to Pila to tell him: That we
protest — that we are neutral — and for that reason —
they might pass? — — —

Karlo:
Tomo: } We are ready!

The duke (as above):
I said when you start to raise the flag in front of Saint Vlaho:
and around it policemen and soldiers .....

Niksha (mockingly but calmly to Mato):
Oh! che bella festa! — — — Oh! che bella festa![1]

---

[1] Really.
[2] A satirical song of Dubrovnik in the beginning of the 19th. century.

M a t o (the same to Niksha):
Only the candles are missing:

T h e d u k e (bowing slowly to the left and to the right):
And now . . . . . Eccellentissimi — — — come with me! . . . . .
We must show Lauriston whom he is dealing with! — — —
(With his former smile): When they pass through, I shall answer
Antun (laughing to himself): What kind of spirit is this! —
He! — he! — — "We are alive and the devil has not got
us yet!" (Turning around to go and bowing again but deeper to
all the noblemen): My noblemen! — — — (He goes towards
the door. They all bow to him.)

O r s a t (whom up to this moment his nearest friends were trying to
soothe, rushes forth in an instant and closing the big white doors,
he places himself in front of them, firm, great, like Orlando, face
to face to the duke):
No! — — —

A l l (with the most various feelings, in one word):
Orsate!

G j i v o (in a loud voice as if he were to rush upon Orsat):
Let him go! — — —

O r s a t (motionless, glorious like Saint Michael upon the threshold
of paradise in a sonorous, terrible voice):
No! — This is my house! — These are my doors! Here
I am master!

T h e d u k e (trembling, almost frightened but not without somekind
of wretched greatness):
Orsate!   I am your duke! — — —

O r s a t (with infinite sadness):
And because you are my duke, here — — — I kneel to
you! (Rushing up to him he kneels down to him.)

A l l: Ah! — — — rise! Sublime! What kind of a man! . . . . . .
What has happened to him? — — Che charlatano?[1]

---

[1] Oh! What a beautiful festival (a historical saying).
[2] What a comedian?

O r s a t (like above, his words are now weeping now fire and crying
the last cry for liberty):
— — — and behold I kiss your cloak as I kissed my dead
mother and I say to you: Master! Don't listen to us and
our wickedness, don't look at our miserable emaciated
faces, — — — think it over at the fatal moment as if we
were not your equals, no, your slaves, your servants.

G j i v o (beside himself, is running between the noblemen):
Well listen to that . . . . he is abusing the noblemen! — — —

O r s a t (getting taller, more fatal as if wanting to melt with the fire
of the word the frost that is freezing all the souls):
— — — and think, we have forgotten everything our ancestors had done since they fled to these rocks, and that
our soul is dead, and we do not know any more who had
been our sages, our poets, our men of the sea, our
martyrs, who made an altar out of this nest, who saved
the face of our enslaved nation! (More and more piercingly
as if clutching the cross of salvation till all faces, all hands, all
sighs tremble and flare around him.) And say in the depth of
your soul that we are the last remnants of a very old,
chosen race, without will, without blood, without brains —
And when you recognize all this, duke, say only one
word, — — — only one . . . .

T h e d u k e (involuntarily, all confused, not understanding anything,
looking all around as if trying to find an explanation to this madness):
Which? — — — which? . . . .

O r s a t (still on his knees, with his ultimate prayer, in his voice and
in his whole being):
I am the master! — — —

A l l (in great confusion, in the greatest contradiction of expressions):
Passionate! immense! — — — Orsate! — — — Keep quiet.
Speak! — — — speak! . . .

O r s a t (slowly rising as if transformed):
And command to have the bridge raised, proclaim that
there are no noblemen, that the people are alone and
you are alone! Shut up all of us, ring the big bell of Our

Lady — and sit down, master, under the arches of your
palace with your people — and be if you like Marin
Faliero .... only save us our Republic, — — — save it
from the foreigner, — save it — — — from us ....

Gjivo (like a tiger):
And we stand such abuses! ....

All followers of Gjivo: To the palace! — — — to the
palace — the Senate is Master! — — — the Senate!

All followers of Orsat (crowding around him, anxious to
bring him back to his right mind which even they suppose to
be darkened):
Orsate! — — — Orsate! ...... get back to yourself! It
is in vain! — — —

Orsat (looking straight ahead with an awful, staring look, tearing
away to free himself from all of them):
I am alive! alive! alive! do you hear! .... (Looking at the
duke as if noticing him for the first time): Why is he red?
Why? When he has no more of the warm blood which
washes away all sins. When he has no tears, no pains, —
when all is perishing in filth, in shame, in dust — — —
ah! — — — (he shudders all over as if looking down from a
peak upon vast space): There .... there .... the gates are
opening .... Oh .... how many there are! ... How many!
— — — First the Frenchmen! All gold, plumed hats, flags!
What handsome men! ..... all thirsty for glory, all hungry
for women! — — — And there again there are others, oh
others, ... all worse, all homelier! Miserable, poor, savage!
And they all want to pass through these gates! — — —
They are all laughing, spitting at the black walls, all croaking!
"Where is your crown? Where is your liberty? You too
are like ourselves!" Oh! ... (while passion has overwhelmed
him, the duke leaves accompanied by Tomo and Karlo and Gjivo
and his friends escorting them and remaining in the background
looking on with anger and a sort of a pale smile at Orsat's suffering).

Orsat (as if coming to himself, but the thought which had lifted him
to the height of enthusiasm has changed its tone, and looks at

all of them wondering whether he might find another opening into
the unfeeling souls of the noblemen):
We are still the power! — — — I — — — you — — —
we — — —! We kings! — — We masters! Where we appear
there the emperors follow us! — — — And our ocean, and
our fortress, and our churches — — and the Palace, — —
all these are still here, living — living —! And all this
should disappear! — and that our children should forget
the meaning of liberty — — and go out into the world
seeking for our name, our rights, our power, and they don't
know that this is a state — — a state! — — — and all the
rest slaves, mere slaves!.... (looking from one to the other
one with the gay enthusiasm of youth, but still his eyes questioning
full of suspicion and fear that his words are powerless, useless):
And if this land of liberty for thousands of years must
perish, let us go brethren, — — children! There are our
ships in the harbor. Let's embark and carry along the flag
of Saint Vlaho, let us sail away like our forefathers have
done! Oh — what a happy sail! Let's go! Let's go! The
sea-gulls and clouds will ask us: Who are you? Whom
are you looking for?... and the sails will answer. Dubrovnik
is sailing! — — Dubrovnik is seeking again the barren rock
to hide his liberty. Show it to us, oh ye clouds! Take us
to the mild Greek country, to the land of the gods! (They all
have come nearer. All are excited, moved. Some have tears in their
eyes. Gjivo involuntarily shivers): Oh! (full of heavenly delight,
as if the words turned into action): Oh! — — — blessed be
those tears! — — — quick, quick — — run — — keep back
the keys. — — — Oh — — saved — — — saved — — —
(the reverberation from a cannon is heard).

All (startling):
What is this? — — — The cannons are shooting!......

Gjivo (somewhat embarrassed):
This is a sign......

Orsat (with a terrible suspicion):
A sign? — — a sign? — — and the duke? — — — and
Karlo? — — — and Tomo? — — where are they — — —

(Noticing the malicious smile of Gjivo who leaning upon his cane is rocking himself carelessly): Ah! — — (he understands) Traitors! — — (He wants to rush upon him but his friends hold him back.)

Gjivo (coldly, deeply, naturally, like another man):
You can't complain, Orsate, — — — we let you say all you wanted to! (To the others like a man of affairs.) The first sign, mi capite.) Lauriston receives our ambassadors — — —. (The second cannon! A pause full of fatal silence. Gjivo continues in a low tone as if talking to himself): And . . . . the second! — — The French are entering.

All (in speechless amazement, fear, uncertainty and liberation):
Ah! . . . .

Orsat (controlling himself with superhuman force, like a figure cast in bronze he remains standing alone, motionless in the middle of the room. One hardly feels from the maddening fire of his eyes, from the twitching of his mouth, from the terrible coldness of his voice, — that a tempest of passion is sweeping across his soul, but that he is the master of the tempest. In a natural voice, with a scornful smile, with great nobility he turns to all groups, and gallantly waving his hand as if saluting them and taking leave of them all):
Yes! Excuse me for keeping you, I did not think it was already all in vain!

Niko
Marko
Luksha
Mato
(they all reach out their hands to him, they all look into his eyes, they all want to embrace. to kiss him, but his soul is strange to them all):
Oh — — our Orsat! — — What shall we do now?

Orsat (as above looking at them from his height with utmost irony):
Since we did not chop off their heads! — — (Closing his eyes for an instant with infinite pain.) Go! — — — Go! — — — leave me alone . . .

Gjivo (coming nearer to him, embarrassed, almost goodnatured):
You know — — — now when all is over — — — let us forget everything — —

Orsat (stabbing him with his look, in a low tone so that his voice is hissing through his half opened lips):

Get out! — — — this minute! don't let me see you again!
(Gjivo as if wanting to flare up.) You are in my house — — —
did you understand! ......

Gjivo (his eyes flaring, mumbling as if to himself):
A family of charlatans! (They go away.)

Niksha (with a fine irony putting the book in his bosom):
I am anxious, Orsate, what kind of faces we shall have
when we wake to morrow!?

Orsat (as above):
Unfortunately! — — — the same ....

Mato
Luco.
Vlagj
Palo
Jero
Luko

(gradually they move away squeezing quietly Orsat's hand
and leave talking in a low tone):
Veramente he speaks beautifully! Although a little
bit theatrically! But how tedious he is! He is not
one of the noblemen! — — — I am sorry for him!
— — — And with all that we shan't be on time to
see the general just as exalted as his late mother!

Shishko (who had been sleeping all through the scene, lazy, stuck
up; going away to Miho):
It is certain that Napoleon will abolish the fee simple?

Miho: Saperlotte! — and immediately! ....

Shishko (casting an angry, scornful look at Orsat):
What is he troubling about, them? — — — (They leave.)

Luksha (going away with a bitter smile to Niksha):
And do you know how all this will come about? Con un
ballo all ungherese[1] he! — it will — it will! — (They go. By
and by they all disappear. The big white doors remain open with
the black gap of the speechless room.)

Orsat the Great (alone.) (Pale, broken down, his throat choking
him, his hair standing up, has dragged himself to the big open
doors looking all around with a kind of empty crazy look. He is
listening to the last steps of those who are going away, to the
gay noise of the street, to the twittering of the sea-swallows — —

[1] A historical, prophetical sentence of Count Luksha Gozze:
That we shall dance to Hungarian fashion.

and all his grief is mounting to his mouth. In vain his strength, in vain his will-power. Something is stifling him. In a heavy, subdued, quivering voice):

No — — — no — — — I won't! — — — Everything is over — — — everything! (With a loud outcry when all strength gives out, vanishes): Woe to me! — — — mother mine! — — — (With his large body falling upon the chair next to the little table he hides his face behind his arm like a child and trembles all over from unrestrainable weeping. In the stillness of the dead house only his sad sobbing is heard like the wailing of a slaughtered beast. In the black air of the open doors looms up like out of darkness the apparition of a woman.)

D e s h a (immovable as if upon the threshold of death she stops, dark, full of secrecy. The long black gown falling in even folds down her tall figure is covering her with a cloak of mourning. A white, transparent fichu à la Marie Antoinette fastened round her short waist reveals her lovely curved white neck, while out of short black sleeves her beautiful white arms are shining, Fair, brilliant hair slightly powdered crowns her head with a kind of tragical reflection. Even her face with its long, statuary curves and the proud lines around her tightly pressed lips, her deep blue eyes and that white curve — — — all this reminds of Delaroche's Marie Antoinette especially now when she is standing there as fatal as inevitable destiny. Pale, calm, cool, with a look of secrecy — she remains looking, looking at the ruin of a man — — at Orsat the Great. A prayerbook in one hand, a handkerchief in the other, both drop down her figure).

O r s a t (raises his head, his face appears dissolved from great pain. Shaking his head dispairingly he throws it back leaning upon his clenched fist):

Nothing, nothing! Neither my prayers — nor my curses, neither my weeping! — Oh! what shame — Orsat is weeping! .... Orsat! Nothing — — — helped! .... They are flying, flying, whirling around the fire! Yes! there are no more wings! .... Frozen souls! — — — empty hearts! Not even reason ..... nor interest — — nor fear! (Getting rigid as if he saw them all before him.) Not even the kind of pride covering their miserable bones until now! ...... I still see them ... and thus I shall see them till doom'sday — — (With horror) : Oh how small they were — — — how empty! — — — How they hated me for seeing their coarse hidden thoughts creeping

over their foreheads and they do not dare to utter them.
— — — Oh! — — — and their eyes, their silence, their
smiles! All that was saying, crying: "What are you
holding us! — — — What are you undressing us! . . . . .
We are naked, naked!" Oh! (shaking all over with misery and
fixing his gaze into distance with a far off voice) and I fool I
thought — what? — that my word could make the dead
alive . . . . (with a still more staring gaze) Lazare! . . . . Lazare! . . . .
(Rising slowly as if entranced. His hands buried into his hair.
The sun is setting. It is striking the seventh hour. He does not
hear it. The warm glow of the sun is shining upon him from one
side. As if in a dream): Not even He — Christ could melt
their icy souls! Not even He! . . . . (Shaking his head he shivers
involuntarily. His consciousness returns and with all the misery
of wretched, inexorable reality. His voice is going out): Strange!
— — — how is it that I am so cold. (Looking around. Only
the sea-swallows are screaming before retiring to rest.) Alone!
— — — alone! — — — They all left me, as if I were to
blame for everything. Even She! — — — my longed-for
love . . . . Firm, big heart, the only human being! — — —
my only faith — — — even She — — —

D e s h a (still in the same place, in the same position, getting paler):
I am here!

O r s a t (at once turns around and remains entranced before her
apparition. Pause. Looking long into each other's troubled face,
then softly):
Oh! — — — how pale you are.

D e s h a (catching hold of the threshold with one hand):
I saw death (she wants to move).

O r s a t (as above quickly, almost praying):
Oh! don't move! — — — You are coming out of the depth
of my desires! — — — (Lower and lower not turning his eyes
from her.) You are as beautiful as death! — and proud! —
The same scornful mouth not meant to be kissed, and those
same overwhite marble hands plucking the flowers of life.
(In a kind of desperate calm): You are, you are the only one
to be here now to look at me to calm me . . . .

Desha (stepping towards him she catches hold of both his hands looking deep into his dim eyes):
I — — — or — — — she?

Orsat (in a subdued tone, broken down, snatching away his hands):
And why did you come then!

Desha (leaning slowly on his shoulder. The last sunbeams are illuminating them with a kind of bloody light. In a low voice, deeply pointing to the sunset burning in the frame of the window):
Don't you see — — —

Orsat (exclaming, grasping her hand and gazing at the setting sun):
Ah! — — — the sun is setting!

Desha: The sun of liberty! — — — (almost embracing each other, speechless they stand in front of the open balcony.)

Orsat (in the great stillness):
How quietly it is setting? . . . .

Desha (leaning her head on his shoulder):
Will it ever come back?

Orsat (as above, in a very low tone):
This, — — — never!

Desha (turning entirely towards the sun as if scorched from looking):
Look — — — look! — — — a little while — — — one more ray — — —

Orsat (as in a dream):
Still — — — still . . . . .

Desha (releasing herself from him steps forward towards the sun, her hands folded as if praying).

Orsat (clutching at her shoulders with both his hands, he buries his head into her shoulders and only one breath comes out from his transformed face. The sun has set):
Ah! . . . .

Desha (making the sign of the cross she presses close to him. A kind of chill passes through her body. Very, very low as if frightened):
· It is no more!! — — —

O r s a t (coming forward, all scowling in thoughts, but quiet):
> When it rises to morrow it will not recognize us any more!
> (A distant big noise and singing as if from an immense multitude.)

D e s h a (going nearer to the window, she startles and quickly looks at Orsat, — — — and as if wanting to close the windows):
> Ah! Oh my Lord!

O r s a t (rises and looks at her. They understand each other. Deathly sweat has broken out on his forehead, there is no more glow, no more anger nor flame in it. — — — The sun has set! — — — Bitterness and grief have slowly glided into him like night. He is breathing quietly but slowly):
> It is they! — — —

D e s h a (frightened, she retreats from the window—pointing her trembling hand into the distance):
> They — — — they — — —

O r s a t (sitting down again, in a very low voice as if calling out into the night):
> Come! — — — here! near me! (The song is coming nearer.)

D e s h a (coming close to him she cowers upon the ground as if kneeling, he encircles her as if wanting to hide her in his embrace. With stifled wrath):
> Cursed song!

O r s a t (as above):
> Ah! don't curse! . . . . . listen! . . . . . (and then the song of the revolution soars up exalted, triumphant into the twilight. A whole army is singing it. All the pigeons, all the sea-swallows wake up and frightened they flutter above the city. Those two miserable people press closer and closer, and as if exalted by the heavenly sound, they involuntarily rise, and remain embraced as if modelled into one cast. Hot tears slowly creep down Desha's face. Gradually the song is dying away as if the army were turning into another street).

O r s a t (entranced by the glorious song, sadly shaking his head, whispers):
> Oh! — — how beautiful it is!

D e s h a: Do you know it?

O r s a t: I heard it in Paris, — while the king's head was being chopped off! (lost in thoughts, in a lower voice) as ours today! . . . . .

D e s h a (her glance fixed as if upon an abyss. The song entirely vanishes in the distance. In a low tone, full of secrecy, almost to herself):
What are we now, Orsate? . . . . .

O r s a t: Slaves.

D e s h a (involuntarily retreating, all full of horror she cries out):
Oh! . . . . . then no! . . . . .

O r s a t (amazed):
What is the matter with you?

D e s h a (looking deep into his eyes):
I am thinking, — — — shall we ever be happy after this hour?

O r s a t: Maybe, — — — if we forget!

D e s h a (going away from him, dark, full of secrecy):
And who could do so?

O r s a t (rushing up to her, grasps her ardently):
You are leaving me?

D e s h a (pale, exhausted, but firm):
No.

O r s a t (holding her hands and looking piercingly at her):
How much grief! — — — how much misery! — — — and now we have reached the threshold of our wretched happiness . . . . .

D e s h a (mouth upon mouth, eye upon eye):
I love you! . . . . .

O r s a t (in terrible doubt gets hold of her face with both his hands and looks at her like Edip at the Sphinx):
Why don't you want then? (Closing her lips with his hands):
Yes! — — — yes! . . . . . I see it in your eyes — — — on your mouth! You won't! — — — Ah and why? . . . . .

D e s h a (putting all herself in to these words): Will our children be — — — as we are — — — Slaves? . . .

O r s a t (calmly, hoarsely releasing his hold upon Desha cutting deep into the misery of these words):
They will! . . .

Desha (whispering, bewitching and terrible):

Then, — — — choose! — — —

Orsat (turning around stands frightened before her, inspired, full of horror and full of grief. As if to himself):

Too sad — too — sweet too great one — like death! (In one stride he rushes upon her, grasps her, presses her to his breast joining lips to lips with a long, passionate kiss. They stretch as if exhausted, separate, he almost turned to stone, sad but as if upon the height of incomprehensible peace, briefly, manly): No!

Desha (squeezing his hand, as pale as death takes her prayerbook and goes towards the doors. When she reaches them she turns around asking simply in a kind of tired way):

Shall I close them?

Orsat (leaning upon the table and incessantly looking at Desha. He shrugs his shoulders, and with a bitter smile):

They don't close them where the dead are. (She waves with her heavy hand as if crossing the threshold of death she were saluting those who stayed on the other shore of the dark river of life. And she goes. Orsat nods his head slowly falling upon the table, broken down, speechless.)

The voice of the milkwoman (down the street):

Milk — women! . . .

The voice of Madam Ane (from the room to the left):

Lucia! — — — Lucia!

Orsat (hearing and understanding the sounds of eternal life he crosses his hands across his breast, and shaking his head whispers to himself):

And now? — — — (Remains lost in thoughts.)

The voice of the milkwoman (losing itself into the merry noise of the revived street, far away, drawling out):

Milk, women! — — —

(C u r t a i n.)

THE SECOND PART OF THE TRILOGY

AFTERGLOW

AFTERGLOW.

Characters:

Mara Mikshina Benesha (68 years old), vladika of Dubrovnik.
Made (42 years) ⎫
Ore   (36 years) ⎬ her daughters.
Pavle (27 years) ⎭
Kata (60 years), a servant of Mara.
Luco Orsatov Volzo (78 years)   ⎫ noblemen of Dubrovnik.
Sabo Shishkov Prokulo (62 years) ⎭
Lujo Lasich (32 years), a navy captain.
Vaso (40 years), a merchant.
A "kozica" (young servant girl).

(The scene takes place in the house of Benesha
[on the Pustijerna] in the City 1832.)

A room of Madam Mara. Poor, old furniture, dusty pictures of old noblemen are hanging on the walls. In the background and to the left of the stage there are doors. To the right a large gothic balcony, half open. Through it across this deserted stillness the last glow of the setting sun is creeping accompanied by the sound of the bells saluting Our Lady.

M a d a m   M a r a (alone). (Is watching the twilight leaning back in a large leather chair. One hand placed on the little table full of wool, lawn and ribbons, she is telling her beads with the other one. She is dressed in an old black gown. White locks are escaping under the little cap she is wearing on her head. According to the fashion of the ladies in the twenties she has thrown a green crepon shawl across her shoulders. Everything upon her is comme il faut, elegant, but very old. Upon her pale, withered face there is a great expression of weariness and nobility. While the bells are ringing, Mara is praying looking into the sunset. When finally the echo stops, she sighs and shrugging her shoulders it is evident she is counting something and that this calculation is troubling her. Again she looks into the sunset, again she sighs): How quickly the sun is setting! — — (Following her former secret thought.) What was it — — did we sell sixteen pints for 45 or 40? — Made said something about altogether amounting to 12, — — no 14 talirs. Yes! — — — yes! . . . . (She wants to go on with her prayer but doesn't feel like it.) Ah! If it should only occur to Vaso to bring me at least half of it! Oh! If he knew . . . . . . if he knew! (Praying more quickly as if afraid): "Holy Mary, Mother of God, pray for us." — — — Oh! Yes, just so — — pray for us! Not a rooster from the peasant nor a hip more than the agreement permits us. Just so! . . . . The olives have dried up and the house in Cavtat is empty. It is true captain Lujo wanted to buy it, but I said: What? . . . . he should think it over. "She invited me to a party! Yes?! — — —

So that I should pay her coffee. (Making the sign of the cross.)
I should say, only this was wanted. (Shaking her head she
looks into the sunset with a kind of dull resignation.)

K a t a (an old maid. Dressed after the fashion in noblemen's houses.
A white kerchief wound around her neck is crossing on her breast;
white stockings are peeping out under her short dark dress. Her
slippers as well as her pleated skirt are hemmed with green tape.
Her hair is braided country fashion under a black headwear. She
enters quickly as if looking for something):
Where for heaven's sake has she hidden herself? — — —
(Noticing Mara she stops, making the sign of the cross.) In the
name of Our Father and — — — Here she is! — —.— and
what did I say?

M a r a (waking up from her thoughts):
Is that you, Kata?

K a t a (shaking her head as if cross, but full of care and kindness):
You just want to catch cold, don't you? Ah?!..

M a r a (ill-humored):
Oh — — oh! Did you begin?......

K a t a: Before the day of Our Lady Nunciata with open windows? — — Did any one ever see that?.....

M a r a (as above): Et ne nos inducas in tentationem!

K a t a: Maybe it is as you say. — but — where there is no
health there is no Latin (closing the window). — — Here
you are!

M a r a (looking at her frowningly and shaking her head):
Kata! — Kata! I hope it is not going to choke you ......

K a t a: Let it, only that my lady keeps alive.

M a r a (rolling back into her chair):
Alas! Here she is now getting out her sentiments.

K a t a (following in a low voice close to her):
— — — because what shall we do later without her?

M a r a (closing her eyes whispers):
Later?! — — — Later?! — — —

Kata (as above, embarrassed to express what she thinks): ˙
Eh! .... they say — that later might be tomorrow.

Mara (startled, she looks into her face):
Tomorrow? — — — what is tomorrow?

Kata: Tomorrow is (quickly) — dinner ....

Mara: Dinner?

Kata (goodnatured, not to frighten her mistress too much):
Is it Tuesday to-day? — — — Yes! And did you give me
20 cents a day before yesterday? Yes. Well then?! .....
All this means I need money for food expenses.

Mara (embarrassed and angry):
All right, all right! ..... When the girls come back from
"the novene" [1] they will give it to you. You know that
mistress Made keeps the keys.

Kata (goes towards the door as if wanting to go out, murmers somehow indifferently):
I know, I know! But meanwhile they, to have — — —

Mara (quickly turning on her):
What?

Kata: They have said: Mother will give it to you.

Mara: Ah! (shivering a little and contracting her shoulders as if a
chill had passed over her. But only for a minute. She immediately
straightens up, rises and with great composure to Kata): If they
said so — — — it must be so. Remind me tomorrow morning
of giving it to you.

Kata: (stopping at the door and squeezing her hands as if in pain
she looks at Madam Mara. To herself):
Ah! My poor miserable lady! ....

Mara: Don't you hear, they are knocking? Go and open; it
will be the girls.

Kata: I am going, I am going. (Withdrawing lazily still shaking
her head.)

---

[1] Pious prayers coming 9 times a day.

M a r a (left lost in thoughts and speechless, she passes her hands over her face, with infinite weariness in a low tone):
We are dying! . . . . . dying! . . . . . and all in vain! Silver, jewels, rings all is sold, pawned! . . . . We have got to find it! We have got to live! — — — (She startles but immediately controls herself as she hears somebody coming up the steps. Brushing her eyes quickly with her handkerchief she sits down in the chair arranging her cap and shawl so her motion would not be noticed): God forgive me, they would say I was crying!

M a d e, O r e, P a v l e (they enter one after the other one, all three dressed alike as it was the fashion in 1830. Big closed hats, wide sleeves and wide dresses. They are wearing wraps of blue crepon. Their skirts are short and their shoes open showing their white stockings. Each one is holding a prayerbook and a white handkerchief in her hand. All three are a little bit stiff and serious. Nothing funny about them but it is evident they are living outside the world. A little servant girl accompanies them and as they enter she remains at the door):

M a d e
O r e (one entering after the other one they go up to their mother and with one motion all three bow low to her):
P a v l e
Madam mother!

M a r a (charmingly leaning back in her chair, half jokingly with a kind of imperial amiability she receives their salutation like a queen bowing to the ladies of the court):
Welcome to me! . . . Welcome to me! Just see how beautiful they are to-day: Really, Made, your hat . . .

M a d e (happily, but with a kind of restrained expression):
If you could have seen how they looked at me! . . .

M a r a (as above):
Oh! Nobody wears a shawl like my Ore.

O r e (bowing low and smiling):
I learned it from you, Madame la Contesse Marina de Benessa, dame d'honneur de S. M. L'Impératrice Marie-Caroline!

M a r a (jokingly and indifferently, caressing the white curls):
Dear me! You, too, have your head full of French . . .

Made: Why shouldn't I? We saw you dancing a contradance with the emperor ...

Pavle (who has handed over her shawl and hat to the little servant girl, imitating them ironically):
Oh! what times! ... what times!

Mara (looking quietly at her):
Always good for well-behaved children.

Ore (in a low tone to Pavle while going away her hat in her hand):
Do you understand?

Pavle (looks quietly at her, shrugs her shoulders, then turns her back on her):
No.

Made (to Ore):
Let's go and change, Ore. (They go and the little servant follows them.)

Mara (turning around she looks kind of amused at Pavle):
You are ill-humored to-day, my philosopher — — — Come here! — Let me see you. (Pavle sits down on a low stool close to her mother and resting upon the arm of the little chair she gazes a long time at her mother's grey hair): Oh! Oh! ... What are those eyes of yours saying?

Pavle (weary):
That they have seen the first sea-swallows to-day, mother.

Mara (smiling):
So early?! ...

Pavle: Ten days earlier than last year.

Mara: You only remember that, Pavle!

Pavle (leaning over with her head, as if in a dream):
I am always waiting for spring, as if something were to happen.

Mara (looking deeper into her eyes, raises her head to see her better):
Is it therefore that your eyes look like crying? ...

P a v l e (startling and getting up hastily, then stopping and frowning):
Yes, it will be therefore and because of something else.

M a r a (surprised):
Kidlet! At your age, in our position .... I should like to know what you are lacking.

P a v l e (bitterly):
Nothing, mother, — and everything.

M a r a:
What kind of words are those?!

P a v l e (quickly getting down at her feet again and whispering close to her, as if afraid of hearing herself):
Scold me, mother, scold me! We are alone. — Nobody sees, — no — nobody hears our weakness. I can confess to you, Madam mother as I should confess to our Master the Lord (sitting down besides her as before, still closer, still lower):
I am afraid! . . . . .

M a r a (moved but amazed):
Afraid?! . . . . .

P a v l e (as above, always quicker and lower):
Slowly, slowly ruin crawled into our miserable house. We are poor. No more treasure — pretty soon no more fireplace. Those dear hands of yours do not spin gold any more, do not wind silk (snatching her mother's hands she kisses them convulsively). About money . . . . about money you trouble! (Hiding her face she begins to cry.)

M a r a (rises all shaken. Her mouth twitches with pain; she, too, would like to cry at all this misery, but all this passes away in an instant and she is firm again):
Who taught you, Pavle, to ask for what our ancestors did not want to?

P a v l e (rises quietly wringing her hands, lifting her face upon which something like anger is vibrating. To herself):
Always the same! — — — Always the same! — — —

M a r a (as above):
> Since when don't noblemen feel proud of their misery, too? If Dubrovnik is enslaved, let us be in grief, too. Do you understand, Pavle?

P a v l e (gazing indifferently upon the ground, she answers indolently):
> I understand.

M a r a (sitting down on the chair arranging her curls and her shawl):
> We have been ruling for thousands of years, it is time for us to die. (A pause. Quietly and mildly.) You will pray tonight, Pavle, a prayer of repentance so that God might free you of vain thoughts.

P a v l e (goes to the window and sits down looking into the darkness which is falling closer and closer):
> I will, mother.

M a d e (peeping in at the door):
> You are in the dark, mother?

M a r a:
> Twilight suits conversation.'

O r e (coming in with Made):
> And grief, too.

M a d e:
> Doesn't Dante say: Era l'ora — — — era l'ora¹. — — Do you remember, mother?

P a v l e (sitting near the window and still looking into the court, deeply as from a distance):
> "Era già l'ora che volge'l desio
> A' naviganti e'ntenerisce il core
> Lo di ch'han detto a'dolci amici addio?"²

M a r a (sadly):
> How beautiful this is! . . . . . .

P a v l e (as above):
> And how sad . . . . . .

---

¹ It was the time.
² It was the time already when the travellers of the sea tenderly remember the parting from their dear friends.

M a d e (calling aloud from the middle door):
Kata! — — Kata! bring in the Roman lamp! (Coming forward.)
Parchè altrimenti[1] we shall melt in poetry.

M a r a: And you, since you like prose so much, Made, here
are two spools of wool for you. Unravel them, let Ore
help you. We must quickly knit some gaiters for Dum
Andro (giving her the spool). You can tire yourself without
a candle.

M a d e (sits down, to Ore):
Ore, hold it! I shall wind it. (Both of them start to work.)
And intanto[2] you might tell me what you had been reading
in the chronicle of Vlagj Benesha. (The whole following conversation is interwoven with the work, everything in a natural
and simple way. Mara is knitting stockings and Pavle getting
some lining ready for charpie.)

M a r a (to Pavle):
Have you anything to do, Pavle?

P a v l e: I am making some charpie out of a lining for the sick.

O r e (to Made, always a little exalted, romantic):
Oh! Made — — he was a nobleman.

M a d e: And how far did you get?

O r e: Where Charles Vth. receives him in audience.

M a d e: Mother! — — do you hear?! ... Charles Vth.!

M a r a: We are still living from the beauty of those days,
daughter dear.

M a d e (in a different tone somewhat angry for not being able to undo
a knot on the spool):
How do you want me to wind when there are too many
knots?

O r e (she, too, is coming down from the Olimp of the past and bends
towards her to help her):
Difatti![3] — — — (calling Pavle) — — Have you any scissors?

---

[1] Because otherwise.
[2] Meanwhile.
[3] In fact.

Pavle (quietly rising approaches her sisters, scissors in hand):
What do you want them for?! (all three girls are busy to
unravel the spool.)

Mara (involuntarily as if remembering something she is gazing upon
her daughters and somewhat absent — minded, plaintively):
They were three doing the same. "Kloto" was spinning!
"Lakezis" was winding the thread — — —

Pavle (as above to her sister):
In vain! It is better to cut of than toil. (She cuts the knot
with the scissors.)

Mara (as above, lost in thoughts and looking at Pavle):
And the third one cuts the thread of life — — — (bent,
leaning on her elbows she is looking straight ahead, involuntarily louder): Well? What was the name of the third
one? — — —

Pavle (turning her head she understands and answers like an echo,
a queer smile upon her lips):
"Atropos", mother! — — — (She sits down at the window again.)

Mara (shivering slightly and leaning on the table, hardly whispering):
Yes! — — — yes! — — — (she begins to knit her stocking
again, shakes her head as if smiling, to herself.) Gracious me.
What crazy thoughts!

Ore: Listen then, what our ancestor, Don Vladislao de Benessa[1],
ambassador of our Republic, is writing. (Still holding the
wool wound around her hand from which Made unwinds the thread
and twists it into a ball. Ore speaks as if she were reading, a
little emphatically for all her nature is inspired with the greatness
of nobility): At first I went into the "salon" of the lance
bearers. There were 25 of them, all in gold and brocade.
Then we went through the salon of the ambassadors
— — — de los embajadores. — — — Here 32 pages with
golden clubs were waiting for us!

---

[1] I have kept the style and language of innumerable similar memoirs which I
found and read in governmental archivs or in the houses of noblemen in Dubrovnik.
In those times Italian was the diplomatic language of Europe just the way French is
now and the State secretaries of all European countries in the XVIth and XVIIth century
were mostly Florentins, therfore the Italian language became with the approval of the
free Republic of Dubrovnik the State language of this Republic. Hence this mixture of
languages in the writing and speech of old Dubrovnik people.

M a r a (to herself):

Ah! — — — If I only had one for — — — tomorrow!

O r e: — — — Then at the doors of the hall del Trono entered el gran mayordomo and calls out: El Rey! And behold a procession as on Corpus Dei and way back in all that gold among halberds and flags one man alone in black with the Toson d'oro[1] on his breast. Wherever he passed everybody bowed to him. It looked like wheat on the fields swayed by a violent wind! They all grew quiet and the man in black mounted the throne and sat down as if tired under the velvet baldachin enbroidered with imperial eagles. That man in black was — — — Carlo Quinto!

M a r a (all trembling with joy she exclaims):

Ah! — — — Carlo Quinto! — — —

O r e (continues without stopping her work):

— — — and then el gran mayordomo quasi[2] on his knees before him whispered something into his ear. Sicuro[3] he was speaking to him about me for the emperor looked at me for a moment with his dim eyes, saluted me and uttered slowly as if he were talking through his nose clearly those two famous words:[4] Cubrias Vos![5] — — — and I covered myself! (Deep night. Ore stops as if inspired and crushed by this memory.) Ah! — — — Mother! did you hear? Carlo Quinto told us . . . .

M a d e ⎱ (in one voice):
O r e   ⎰

Cubrias Vos!

M a r a: Eh! . . . . children! — — — we dearly paid for that hat!

P a v l e (growlingly plucking the charpie):

"Three hundred widows by the name of Vica!"

---

[1] Golden Fleece.
[2] Almost.
[3] Surely.
[4] Cover yourself!
[5] There is a legend about 300 widows by the name of Vica having been left on the island of Lopud alone after the destruction of the imperial fleet which Charles Vth had sent against Algir, ruined by a tempest. Our famous Antun Casali wrote a great poem on this subject.

Made (going on with her work):
You may say what you like, I am still dazzled by so much splendor.

Kata (entering from the middle door with a lighted Roman lamp which she is holding high and carrying it to the little table): Bonasera!

All the ladies: Bonasera! — — —

Kata (putting the candle on the little table):
We don't have any more wicks in the house, Madam.

Pavle (laughing, ironically to Ore and Made):
Are you dazzled by this kind of glory, too?

Made (shocked):
Pavle! — — — —

Ore (equally scornful):
Some people already call you: "Pavle Jacobina"!

Pavle (quietly rising):
It is a pity I am not.

Kata (to Mara):
Captain Lujo sent a message be was coming to say good bye tonight.

Pavle (in a suppressed tone to herself):
Ah! — — — —

Mara: I am sorry for him.

Kata: He said: I must be going.

Made ⎞ (working, indifferently):
Ore ⎠
Let him go!

Pavle (crushed, she sits down as before, to herself):
Everything comes to an end — — — everything!

Kata (at the door remembering something and turning to Mara):
Here! — — I forget everything, Madam! Eh! so many years! Will you see Vaso?

Mara (surprised, almost joyfully):
  What? Vaso? Has he come?!......

Kata: Poor man he has been waiting downstairs in the little parlor.

Made⎱ (as above):
Ore ⎰
  Let him wait!

Mara (to herself):
  Oh! Those are my prayers! — — —

Kata (to herself):
  If she knew I had sent for him! — — —

Mara (indifferently to Made leaning comfortably back into her chair):
  How much did you agree upon for a pint of cotognata[1], Made?

Made: For twenty and a half.

Mara (adding up in her head):
  Yes..... so it is. (to Kata): Tell him to help himself.

Kata (goes out shaking her head):
  In vain! Who is a nobleman, is a nobleman!

Made (gets up, puts away her work and approaching her mother says in kind of a solemn way):
  Don't forget, mother, that Vaso, the Herzegovac[2] bought the house of your nono[3] Tudizich at the auction. (She goes).

Ore (the same as Made):
  — — — and that our peasants call him: Master Vaso!
  (She goes.)

Pavle (whispering to her mother in a low tone):
  Thank him mother. (She goes.)

Mara (gazing after Pavle):
  It seems to me: Pavle has a reason!

[1] Quince preserves.
[2] Man from Herzegovina.
[3] Grandfather.

V a s o (enters, takes the fez of his head, bows low. Stopping at the entry):
Madam!

M a r a (seated, without turning):
Oh! Is it you Vaso! — — Bravo, yes! Welcome here!

V a s o (coming nearer slowly as if treading upon beads):
Eh! thank you, Madam (he kisses her hands). Here I am; — — and how is your health, Madam?

M a r a (with great amiability but with an unspeakable expression of inner greatness):
Old age, Vaso mine! — — — And how is Angja? — — —
I heard she has given happy birth.

V a s o (blissfully):
How kind you are, Madam! — — upon my faith she bore me a hero!

M a r a (looking at him smilingly as if trying to find the reason for his coming):
And what did you come for, Vaso?

V a s o (embarrassed but with a kind of crafty smile turning his fez between his fingers):
Eh! — — — you know — — Vaso is indebted to you, Madam

M a r a (as above):
To me?!......

V a s o (as above):
Eh! — — well, you honestly sold me the cotognata and I, upon my word .... honestly forgot — — — he! he!

M a r a (leaning upon the table as if surprised with an infinite expression of indifference):
My poor Vaso! — — — What did you worry yourself — — — There was really no hurry about it.

V a s o: There was, there was, Madam! — — Well — what do you want? Work! Eh! That your head is turning. I bought a house, a big, empty one, — — — the palace of Tudizich — — — — do you know, Madam?

Mara (reserved but quietly and coldly):
   I don't know, Vaso.

Vaso (encouraged, he tells naively what he feels):
   Eh! if you saw the empty rooms! — Gracious me! As vast
   as mosques, and the walls, dear me, are like those of a
   castle tower, Madam! — — — Ah! What did I get myself
   into such an affair. It will take money to change all this
   into a store-room for flour! (While talking he has got hold
   of a chair where he wants to sit down.)

Mara (getting up slowly and calling quietly):
   Kata! (Simply and frankly to Vaso): You said, I believe,
   16 pints, for? — — —

Vaso (straightening up, with his former embarrassed great humility):
   — — — for 45, Madam! — — for 45! — — —

Kata (entering):
   You called me?

Mara (to Kata):
   You will get money from Vaso. (To Vaso with her former
   kind smile and her fine amiability): You know, she is keeping
   account of such trifles.

Vaso (handing a package of money to Kata):
   Forgive me, Madam, do you want me to count it? — — —

Mara (with great nobility, getting sweeter and sweeter):
   What are you thinking of, Vaso! I am only sorry you
   have been waiting poor man. Think of your neighbor
   sometimes, Vaso! — — and don't forget to remember me
   to Angja! — — —

Vaso (all bent and full of bliss because of so much honor, kisses
   her hands, he leaving backward at the middle door):
   Eh! dear! may your mouth be guilded, Madam! — — —
   I shall come again — — —

Mara (moving her hand with a royal gesture):
   Adio, Vaso!

Vaso: Adio, Madam! (Goes.)

M a r a (to Kata coldly, dryly):
Kata, count it over.

K a t a (having counted):
Not a penny is missing.

M a r a (takes the money and puts it into her pocket, then goes towards her room):
I told you: you will get it tomorrow. (She goes away.)

K a t a (looking after her):
In vain! — — — (She goes shaking her head.) Who is a nobleman! (She goes.)

P a v l e (enters quickly from the lower doors looking restlessly all around not to be seen by her mother — her eyes are dim, her white lips tightly pressed):
I told him to go and he obeyed me. I have been waiting for him eight years, he returned and again he is going away! — — — And I am alone again without comfort, without hope. — Oh! everything passes, — everything falls away! Even youth and those sad days. — — (Coming to the balcony she looks into the court.) One more ray — there upon our Lady — — and then great, long misery . . . . . night! (She is buried in dark thoughts.)

L u j o (coming in through the middle door):
Kata told me she was here (catching sight of Pavle, he stops). Ah! — — she is alone.

P a v l e (coming back to herself she strokes her white forehead with a tired hand):
If there were no thoughts there would be no misery. But thus . . . I need force nothing but force.

L u j o (aloud):
Why?

P a v l e (frightened):
Lujo! — — — you here! — — —

L u j o: You are calling for force: here it is.

P a v l e (sharply):
You were listening?

Lujo (scowling):
    No. I heard — — —

Pavle (embarrassed):
    You came to say good bye to us? Didn't you? Ah! — — —
    you are going — — — I shall call mother.

Lujo (wanting to detain her):
    Wait, Pavle!

Pavle (quickly):
    No — — — no — — — (running to the door on the left she
    quickly calls):
    Mother!

Mara's voice: Who is it?

Pavle (as above):
    Captain Lujo has come. He wants to say good bye to you.

Mara's voice: Here I am! Detain him a moment.

Pavle (Pause. Quiet but exhausted she turns towards Lujo leaning
    on the threshold):
    Have pity with me!

Lujo (approaching her, in a low voice but passionately):
    Am I going this time, too, without hope?

Pavle (quietly wringing her hands and dragging herself to a chair
    she cowers down in it):
    Oh! — — — my grief! — — —

Lujo (close to her, firmly but with deep passion):
    Turn me out, but I must speak — for the first and for the
    last time. (In a lower tone): We were children, I the son of
    a peasant, you the daughter of a duke. And they sent me
    to sea. For years I have been knocking about the world.
    Whether I came or whether I went your eyes and your
    golden hair crowning your forehead were always in my
    mind. I came back, here — — — a man and a "gentleman"
    as foreign, free people are calling me. Wretched me! — — —
    They did not know when I am with you — — — I am
    your slave again!

P a v l e (stopping her mouth with her fist she is looking steadily on the floor):
It is! — — — it is! — — —

L u j o (as above, more and more animated):
My peasant origin has poured into me the lowest kind of humiliation. (Quite low and passionately): My love for you, last noblewoman mine!

P a v l e (getting up quietly, eye to eye, she is looking sharply, piercingly at him):
And who allowed you that?

L u j o (taking convulsively hold of her hand, face to face):
Ah! — because you are higher in your grief than all of us in our happiness, — because, because, — Pavle, I love you — I want you!

P a v l e (snatching away her hand, with desperate courage):
Why are you wasting so many words?

L u j o : You are laughing at me?

P a v l e (quietly, with infinite grief):
I have been listening to you without running away.

L u j o (bitterly):
Then who is snatching you away from me?

P a v l e (as above):
You said: my grief! — — If you are a slave in my house,
I am here a slave of my nobility.

L u j o (taking hold of her hand, sweetly and decidedly):
Let us break the fetters, let us be men, Pavle!

P a v l e (looking at him full of great suffering, deeply afflicted because of her inner sacrifice):
Who moves only one slab out of these cracked walls, destroys our palace, kills our nobility. (With a piercing glance bewitching his sight.) Do you want to? — — —

L u j o (angrily, with inexorable hardness of other longings):
Without heart, — — without heart, — — as all your people!

Pavle (sadly, with a dead look, she smiles leaning upon the little table):
Do you call so those who are dying for their flag?

Lujo (sits down crushed covering his face with his hands):
Pavle! —— Pavle! —— Heavy is this cross!

Pavle (slowly, putting her hand solemnly upon his head):
We are carrying it —— for the sins of others — — —
like our Master, the Lord!

Lujo (startles, gets up, convulsively):
Oh! —— here they come —— —

Pavle (smiling sadly):
—— our noblemen!

Mara (entering the door):
Are you just leaving, Lujo?

Lujo: I am going, Madam, where I came from.

Mara (amiably):
Dubrovnik is small, young man!

Lujo: —— and sad.

Mara (in her chair, sighing):
Eh! — —— What do you want? —— — Too full of
recollections!

Ore (coming in):
Don't forget to bring my parrots, Lujo.

Made (coming in after her):
And what will you bring me? (Speaking to him.)

Ore (coming close to Pavle, in a low voice, quite indifferently):
How will you do without him?

Pavle (shrugging her shoulders, in the same low tone):
As before.

Ore: The better for you. (Going away from her, still in a lower tone):
Remember Maria-Orsola.

Pavle (remaining for a moment as if struck):
Maria-Orsola! —— —

K a t a (at the door):

Master Luco and Master Sabo have come to see you.

M a r a (rising):

Finalmente![1] (To Kata): Receive them and bring the coffee. (Kata goes out.)

O r e: Che fortuna![2] — —⁓— how long since our noble duke has not been here.

L u j o: What? Master Luco?

M a r a (half grieved):

The only living nobleman who was once our ruler.

L u c o (is seen at the door panting, all out of breath from asthma and from the high stairs. Stout, puffed up with pride, on feeble legs, he hardly moves leaning upon a big gold-handled cane. He is dressed à la vieux régime wearing open shoes and a dark blue frock coat with golden buttons, a large black tie round his neck. Upon his head he has a black velvet cap which he never lifts His face is shaved. He is wrapped in a cloak[3]. Everything on him is simple and clean. He enters lazily as if his legs were unable to stand the weight of his overheavy body. His speech is a mixture of incomprehensible mumbling and loud puffing. Great age, great weakness, great nobility):

Uf! — — — these cursed stairs!

M a r a (meeting him):

Welcome to us! Ma bravo, Luco! Dunque[4] your legs are getting well again?

L u c o (sinking down upon the sofa):

Che[5] — getting well — They are worse! — worse!

S a b o (coming in after him. Thin, rigid, small, dressed à la 1820 poorly but exquisitely with a kind of elegancy. He moves automatically his hands behind his back, his eyes closed, his face like a hard parchment. He is ridiculous, but the emphasized grand-seigneur. Everything in him is pride. He does not look, he does not turn, but in a kind of infinite moral indolence, for all that is presence

---

[1] Finally.
[2] What good fortune!
[3] An oldfashioned broadcloth wrap (manteau).
[4] Well then.
[5] Usual Italian interjection: What.

has closed his mouth, only growling at times. Whether he speaks
or whether he keeps quiet the same expression of scorn is drawn
across his lips. He has neither hat nor wrap. Coming to the
middle of the room he nods saluting the ladies, waving his hand
then stops, crosses his hands behind his back, closes his eyes
and laughs aloud; one might say: the crows are croaking):

Made! — — — Ore! — — — He! He! . . . . .

The Ladies: Welcome to us, Sabo!

Sabo (immovable in the middle of the room, croaks again):
He! He!

Ore:
Made: } What's happened to you?

Sabo (as above):
Did we bet, si or no!

Ore:
Made: } By all means! (Inquisitively): Dunque?

Sabo (as above):
He! He! He! . . . . . .

¡Ore
Made } (around him): Was it clear, Sabo?

Sabo (closing his eyes, with a kind of malicious satisfaction he is
looking first at the one and then at the other one, pronouncing
syllable after syllable):
It was rain — ing!!

Ore
Made } (jokingly as if they were very much troubled):
Oh! we have lost!

Luco (cross because not understanding):
Where is your rain? — — — Sabo, — where?!

Sabo (as if proclaiming great news, closing his eyes and raising his
eyebrows):
On the day of Saint Vlaho, 1796 . . . . . .

Mara
Luco } (as if cross because of his mockery):
But! Sabo! . . . . .

Sabo (continues paying no attention neither to what they are saying nor to what they are doing):
— — — When the noble Duke Niksha Benesha . . . . . .

Mara (surprised, inquisitive):
My poor Niksha?!

Sabo (as above):
— — — When the noble Duke Niksha Benesha left his palace carrying a wax torch in his hand, it was rain — ing! (Contracting his shoulders, towards Ore and Made, as if pitying them for not knowing.) I read so in my memoir! — E tanto basta! — — —

Ore (handing him upon a little plate a bit of quince jelly and almonds; very amiably and gracefully):
Bets are sweet when Sabo gets them!

Sabo (eyeing quickly what she is giving him, and strocking Ore's face):
Bravo Ore! — he! he! — It will be for my hunger, too

Lujo (to Pavle, in a low voice, watching wonderingly all those apparitions of incomprehensible past ages):
What — is he starving?! — — —

Pavle: He would rather do so than accept a stranger's mercy.

Mara (conversing with Luco):
Sabo guessed right. I remember! — Oh — gracious me, as if it had been yesterday! — — — My poor Niksha — he wanted to go to church in silk stockings. Just imagine! And it began to pour like everything! You won't, Niko, I said to him and I made him pull on two pairs of wool socks and above them silk stockings. Yes!? — and how he obeyed me!

Luco: And at my house Ane! Uf! — — — Crying all the time: you should take your cloak. There will be the ambassadors from Paris and Vienna! Ha! Ha! What shall I do with a cloak when the storm wind is raging and Nikola has broken two window panes in the Senate?! — Uf! — — — Ane quarrelled and I?! — I put under my cloak, you know what? — The hide of a hare! — Ha! Ha! —

A 'Duke in a hide! — — — (From uproarious laughter he begins to cough. He puffs, snorts, and blows his nose with a big blue handkerchief.)

M a r a (laughing):
Ah! If poor Ane could hear us! . . . .

L u j o (in a low voice to Pavle):
And you can live with them! —

P a v l e (with a pale smile):
'And die.

L u j o (in suppressed wrath):
They are not men! — — —

P a v l e (lower and lower):
The nightly light calls the souls to their meeting.

K a t a (carrying upon a tray, coffee, hard bread and cake. She goes to Master Luco and to every one):
Help yourself! I beg you! Do you want some more sugar? Here is some bread. (Everybody takes, drinks, bites. Kata remains in the background waiting for everybody to finish. The following conversation is interwoven with coffee.)

L u c o (to Mara pointing to Lujo):
And who is he?! — — —

M a r a: A navy captain, you know — Lujo Lasich!

L u c o: Lasich! — Lasich! A peasant!

M a r a: His father was one.

S a b o (coming close to Mara):
Then his son is one, too.

M a r a (to Sabo):
Navy people are not peasants, Sabo.

S a b o (scornfully):
Yes, yes! — — — that is a Sorboneze[1] Statement! (Drinking coffee.)

---

[1] Modern views as opposed to the old views of the Salamankezi.

P a v l e (offering some coffee to the navy man in a low tone):
Take the last, Lujo.

L u j o (suppressed angrily):
May it turn into poison!

P a v l e (as above):
Why are you weaker than I?

S a b o (to Mara, scornfully):
And did you receive Madam Fran Matov! He! He! —

M a r a
O r e   } (as if offended):
M a d e
Oh! Sabo — — —

L u c o: And who is that? Who? —

O r e: Dear me, Luco! Don't you know?! Mato Lukov Binciola!
A nobleman of Dubrovnik, ciambellano e Conte dell' Impero,
he married Frana, the daughter of the Greek-Orthodox
Batistich, a shopman in Cavtat.

M a d e (in great horror):
La contesse Françoise!

L u c o (scornfully):
His father was with the French — already! . . . .

M a r a: Veramente[1], I understand everything but that! (Kata has
collected all cups and gone.)

L u j o (restrains himself from flaring up. Pavle controls him with word
and look; in a low voice passionately):
Do you• hear their rotten souls?! — Ah! — Pavle, Pavle!
Come away with me into life.

P a v l e (more and more firmly):
Would you captain leave your sinking ship?

L u j o (waking up, quickly, with instinctive horror):
No!

---

[1] Truly.

P a v l e (with a bitter smile):
You see!

M a r a (rising):
If you want a game?

L u c o (the same):
Let's go, let's go!

L u j o (to Mara):
Madam . . . . . . I am going!

M a r a (very amiably):
Come back to us soon.

O r e : }
M a d e : } Adio, captain!

P a v l e (to herself):
Yes! — — — go, too, as she went . . . . .

L u c o (tottering to the door on the left):
Adio, young man! Adio! (Turning to him.) If you should chance
to meet on the sea the flag — — — you know? — — —
The flag of Saint Vlaho — — — salute it! — — —

S a b o (in a hard voice):
In vain you trouble yourself! — — — It is no more!

L u c o (stops, his mouth open as if terribly surprised):
Ah?! — — — (Getting back to himself, shaking himself, coughing,
he mumbles): Look devil, — — — look! — — —
(Taking Mara's hand.) Even if we are old! (Mumbling.) It is no
more!? (He stops again and once more old thoughts return):
And why is it no more?! Why?! — — — (He goes away
arm in arm with Mara.)

L u j o (to Pavle):
Madam Pavle, I take my leave. (Quickly, in a low voice, bitterly):
I am coming back. And then?

P a v l e (with a deadly smile):
I shall be the old one, Lujo!

L u j o (lower and lower):
I shall love you even in my old age.

P a v l e (as above):
I shall be dead.

L u j o (hoarsely, desperately, face to face):
Then you will be mine!
P a v l e (flaming up, all in a low tone, almost merrily):
Oh! then I shall!

S a b o (to Ore and Made going out):
How merry Pavle is!

M a d e (reserved):
And why shouldn't she?
O r e (taking hold of his hand):
The Senature are calling us to the big council. (They go out
laughingly to the left.)

P a v l e (seeing at the same minute Lujo going out at the middle door.
Fear and despair overwhelm her and she sobs out): Lujo! — — —

L u j o (turns just on the threshold, rushes on to her and passionately grasps her):
Are you coming with me?!

P a v l e (catching his head with both her hands and fixing her gaze
upon him as if she wants to drink him all in and for ever remember his face):
No! — — — Only to see you once more before death.
— — —

L u j o: Pavle! — — —

P a v l e (pushing him away from her):
And now — — — go! (He startles; quickly kisses her upon
her forehead and runs away full of despair.)

P a v l e (stands as if struck by lightening. From the neighboring room
laughter and talking are heard. She catches at her head and with
a maddened look takes in all the emptiness of her surroundings.
Despair seizes her for a moment and in her torturing thought
she runs to the balcony as if wanting to open it and fly away,
then stops exhausted on the threshold): No! (all shivering). To
see him once more — — — Then! — — — then? (Wanting
to open.) "Then you will be mine!" Well, then? Death! — — —

(Drawing back as from an abyss out of which a deep distant thought is growing.) Maria Orsola — — — she too, buried herself to live for one, only one eternal thought. — (A pause.) "Then ..... then. I shall be yours!" (Sobbing deeply she covers her face with her hands. It is a minute. Her firm invincible will which has developed back from historical ages strengthens her to the grandeur of force.) Before the day is dawning — — — Yes — — — At once, at once! Who dies, does not wait! (With a decided step she goes towards the room out of which noise and laughter of the players reach her, but at the door she shudders.) Poor mother! — — — If it were not for her, I should die (calling quietly): Mother! — — — Mother! — — —

Mara (from the inside):
What is it, Pavle?

Pavle: Are you playing?

Mara: Not this minute.

Pavle: Then — — come. Somebody is calling you!

Mara: Here I am, here!

Pavle (growing pale — terror has overcome her. Like a dead soul she is leaning upon the first chair):
Don't leave me, oh my Lord!

Mara (entering at the left door, stops. She does not distinguish anything in the semidarkness):
Who is calling me?

Pavle (immovable, void of feeling):
Maria-Orsola.

Mara (amazed):
Maria-Or — — —, comes up to her daughter looking piercingly at her, trembling.) Did you say so?

Pavle: Yes — — I did.

Mara (snatching convulsively her daugther's hand she leads her to the candle):
Your father's aunt Maria-Orsola Bobali ...... became a nun ...... because she loved — — — a peasant.

Pavle: As I do.

Mara (almost moaning):
    You! —— — You! —— —

Pavle (still void of feeling, hard):
    The man who just left took away all my soul.

Mara (with suppressed anger and scorn):
    You loved a slave?!

Pavle: As if he were a nobleman, mother!

Mara (crushed she sinks into a chair):
    Ah! —— this is the end of everything!

Pavle (coming near her, deeply, as if from a great distance):
    I am sorry for you, mother! But you know it is better
    thus. You are keeping two daughters. I must die to the
    world (she shivers) when I cannot die to life.

Mara (rises looking sharply a long time at her):
    Why now, when he is going?

Pavle: He said: I shall come back!

Mara: Well then?

Pavle (face to face):
    If I see him once again, I am his!

Mara (very low, piercingly):
    Were you waiting for me to tell you: Go with him?

Pavle (quickly turning her head and straightening up):
    You don't believe me! ——

Mara: And why should I?

Pavle (desperately, angrily, scornfully, each of her words like a
    burning fire):
    Why?!.... Why?!.... I have killed joy, stifled youth,
    saved your pride, and why?! My bones are breaking, my
    soul is writhing, and my mother is mocking me: Why?!
    —— — Why?!

M a r a (still harder, still taller):

Maria-Orsola did not say a word! She bent her head and went.

P a v l e (in utmost boldness, all aflame with wrath):

Ah! — to die, and keep quiet! Is that it! So our ancestors bid us! . . . . Impure thoughts are not even allowed to stay over night at the Benesha palace! — Yes . . . it is this torturing you in your great grief! You want the deed and not the words. Well then. . . . . . (Throwing herself like a tiger upon the little table she snatches the scissors and with one movement loosens her long beautiful hair.)

M a r a (understands. She wants to stop her, trembles from fear and emotion):

Dear little daughter, what are you doing — — ah! — — What — — —

P a v l e (with convulsed sort of crazy laughter):

She was called Atropos! — — (In one instant she has cut all of her hair.)

M a r a: Ah! — — — (Screams and sinks back into the chair covering her face with her hands.)

P a v l e (comes to her exhausted but quiet, and like an offering to a speechless deity she kneels down handing to her mother a lock of her cut hair. Slowly, in a low tone deeply):

Maria-Orsola is asking you: do you believe her?

M a r a (opening her hands she presses her daughter upon her bosom, and pride, satisfaction and grief appear in her face):

My dear little daughter! (Noise and laughter are heard from the neighbouring room. Somebody is calling): Come mother! — (The two miserable women remain embraced.)

(C u r t a i n.)

THE THIRD PART OF THE TRILOGY

ON THE TERRACE

ON THE TERRACE.

Characters:

Master Luksha, count Menze (Menchetich), a nobleman
of Dubrovnik ....65 years
Master Niko, his brother.........................70 „
Madam Mare, his sister ....68 „
Ida, their niece ....21 „
Baroness Lidia ....29 „
Madam Slave ....48 „
Emica, her daughter...........................19 „
Madam Lukre...............................52 „
Ore, her daughter ....18 „
Jelka, their friend...........................24 „
Madam Klara...............................60 „
Dum Marin, a priest ....66 „
Count Hans...............................34 „
Baron Josip Lasich ....28 „
Marko de Tudizi, employee.....................36 „
Vuko, a peasant from Konavlje.
Vica, maid in the house of Master Luksha.
Three musicians from the City.
Two girls in Luksha's house.
(The scene takes place in 1900 at the villa of Master Luksha
in Grush.)

(As the curtain rises the stone terrace of the Menchetich villa flooded with sunshine and decorated with the tops of palm-trees, sycamores and blossoming rhododendrons mounting from a park, as spacious as the field dei Signori of some classical Italian little residence, is flaring up suddenly all smiling and spreading gorgeously in length and breath of the stage — quiet, great, dignified in the gold of the first autumnal sunset.

Through the slender Gothic little columns of the furthest parapet there appears far below the terrace the bay of Grush[1] steeped in all the manycolored shades of gold and copper. The magnificent extension of the white terrace would be too cold and empty, if it were not for the rising of Petka[2] with its mild peaks in the background, which mountain viewed from the terrace is somehow rigidly fixed upon the horizon, green, dark, lost in thoughts like the Sphinx of the Syrian deserts. A thick fir tree forest covers its brow coming down in knotty groups on both sides, and spreading a cloak of mild weariness over all the magical unchanged series of historical profiles which are mounting and descending from our Lady of Compassion to the last point of Lapad, and upon which the quiver of the burnt up soul of Dubrovnik is still vibrating.

Out of this mass of green getting darker and darker where not exposed to the sunshine, architectural black silohuettes of Saint Michael's cypresses, those guardians of the dead national power, are looming up like the shadow of a dark Gothic cathedral.

And how small are contrasted with these heights the quiet little houses on the shores of Lapad! The shades of Petka have already flooded them with a kind of violet semidarkness, so they have started to blink sleepily like having grown tired from staring incessantly into the quiet waters bathing their feet in it they are so to say seeking whether the old castle of Guchetich, the secret-bearing Lorko, which recently vanished with all its goodnatured spirits and proud Lombardian windows had possibly sunk into the muddy bay.

But even if the old walls are tumbling down, something is still living, some proud thing growing out of the red moist earth on the cape of Lapad.

---

[1] Pronounce sh in Grush like S in measure.
[2] A mountain.

Cypresses — cypresses, all around cypresses!

Behold there they have ranged themselves near the proud deserted villa of Gjorgjich in a sort of mournful, secret-bearing procession and then again behold them mounting descending, stopping, conversing, getting more and more tired, more and more distracted. They are looking for something lost among the fir trees, olives, among the little dales, something Petka might show them, Petka upon which they are all fixing their veiled black look. Meanwhile upon the Menchetich terrace where the slabs are washed out like marble from the innumerable steps of its dead and living masters, the sun is still throwing all its reddish gold, the doves are still kissing, and the lizards are sticking to the vases in the heraldic position of Pracat's meaning.

There is so much air, light and beauty upon this picture of classical times that one cannot hear the noise of the people passing Grush and enjoying the splendid autumnal sunset.

A low wall with a stone seat closing the terrace from the right is broken through in one place. Here the rhododendrons are the thickest and here are some steps leading into the garden. A little further from this opening rises the tall, carved wall of a magnificent Gothic house, the big arched open gates of which resemble a balcony leading into the dwelling place of Master Luksha.

On the left side the terrace is broken up by a beautiful little house chapel, gently set upon the hard pavement between palm-trees and cypresses. How exquisite and graceful it looks with its closed rennaissance portal and the fine "rosette" carvings, the beautiful font around which the stony leaves of iris and acanthus are wound above the marble angel of Donatello's school who is praying his hands folded on the top of the proud tower of the Menchetich scutcheon.

The crown of this sacred place is a romance belfry, all covered with ivy and white roses embracing the black iron cross on the top and spreading hence all over in wreaths and festoons hiding behind a flowery curtain a litte brass bell, silently peeping upon the sunflooded terrace.

And all these peep look are silent talk and melt into one harmony of lines and feelings. Why shouldn't they, when from time immemorial they have been the same, the bell and the ivy, the terrace and the doves, Petka and the masters.

The masters?

Should Ladies dressed in flowery "guardinfanta"[1] gowns and noblemen wearing wigs or attired after the fashion of ambassadors from Constantinople suddenly step into this enchanted, motionless scene of petrified life, the looker on would observe that possibly nothing had changed in the world, and they still kept praying in the churches from Molunte to Rat:

---

[1] Guardinfanta = big gatherings on the sides in female rococo costumes Louis XVI.

"Domine salvam fac Republicam!"

But who would think that the master of this world of revived
beauty and antiquity is yonder immense human form reclining on the
leather chair, one hand resting upon the little table upon which the
modest priest Dum Marin all curled up is writing, while with his other
hand he is putting a pipe under his grey moustache and bending down
has fixed his eyes upon the ground.

And yet he is the master of this paradise! Master Luksha Menze,
count of Prigorje from the very noble family of Menchetich who had
crowned Dubrovnik with the immortal, angelic diadem of the heavenly
Mincheta[1]. It is really he, the master of innumerable estates, the
experienced diplomat, the model patriot, who in the time of ideal
national struggle defended before the imperial throne the union of his
united nation of one blood, he, the last nobleman poet of Dubrovnik
who has locked up into this magical loneliness his bitter scorn over
the defeat of all national and social ideals?!...

If it were not for his powerful head, for his big, prolongued Titian
forehead, and these deep eyes hiding behind thick brows the unquenched
flame and blame of the past, those superfine hands and that strange,
goodnatured smile upon his hard lips — his heavy awkward, overbig
body and some kind of scornful carelessness as to his coarse old suit,
he would be a sad, dark stain in the midst of glorious reflection and
so many colors.

Just now Master Luksha raises his head fixing his eyes straight
ahead. Oh!... Look here! Yes! Yes!... This face, too, is made of
the same stone, the same sky and the same harmony of nature and
inanimate things. The soul of this man ought to be great, deep and
beautiful like the sunlit scene facing Petka.

But ... Whist!... enough whispering! The play begins.
Listen and judge.)

M a s t e r   L u k s h a (is smoking somehow ill-humoured out of his pipe,
mumbling incomprehensible words as he always does when other
far off thoughts take possession of him. His voice is low, deep
and hoarse as among all of his race. He is dictating or as the
official style 'phrases it telling into the pen of Dum Marin who
is writing upon the little table in the shade near the Gothic doors
of the room wherefrom as usual the daily heat had driven them
out into the yard.)

D u m   M a r i n (close to the little table, he is writing slowly his head
bent, his wide open eyes peeping behind the glasses are following
across his shrivelled nose the pen crawling and squeaking upon
the white paper. All of his wretched face as well as his bald skull,

---

[1] Mincheta = a fortress in Dubrovnik.

bear a somewhat astonished, frightened expression as the unheard of words are stringing out of his trembling pen. Each time when he stops writing a sentence. Master Luksha has thrown at him, the modest writer repeats the last words, every time with another expression, of course as much as the flock of petty thoughts whirling through his dull brains along with his work permit him. For you must know his head is still filled with the uproar and recommendations of the old girl Mara who had been quarrelling this very morning with her neighbor because the "cochinchina" hen of the latter one had jumped into the cabbage of captain Bosho! [oh the blessed cabbage!]. And then the feast of Saint Michael .... is humming again in an empty corner of his frightened mind. And there behold whole processions of "cookies", "wax candles", "bottles", "sermons", "rosolio"[2] are descending, sparkling and merrily playing upon the white paper calling to the miserable writer in whose ears the little bell of Saint Michael's is already tinkling, inviting the fir trees, and cypresses and cyclamens as well as the living and the dead to a treat at the priest's house. Happily Master Luksha is buried in thoughts, his gaze fixed upon his pipe for otherwise Dum Marin would not have understood a word. And sighing he looks at the Master behind his glasses as if God forgive — saying to him: It is easy for you to dictate a book: "Why the noblemen at the end of the 19th century disappeared in Dubrovnik", when your house is full of hens from Shupa[3] and provisions from Ston, and wine! Oh my gracious never like this year! Well, why did they perish! Oh! well! For they neither wanted nor knew how to take care of their own, just like you, my dear Master Luksha, because thus and so, ... and all this is sizzling whistling, boiling in Dum Marin's skull, as if one head caught a humming fly under an empty cup.

And Master Luksha still lost in thoughts is gazing at his pipe, from which not a whiff of smoke comes out any more.

At last Dum Marin gets tired of it. He yells out the last words of Master Luksha in a voice as if singing "Dominus Vobiscum" upon the altar:

...... Without desires, without work. (Thus saying Dum Marin starts to blow as if out of bellows blinking a bit crossways upon the white paper, one might say, the painter is delighting in the charm produced by the last touch of his famous brush.)

Master Luksha (with his hand stuffing the ashes into his pipe, he repeats indifferently):

---

[1] Pronounce **sh** like S in measure.
[2] A kind of liqueur.
[3] Shupa — pronounce **sh** like S in measure.

Yes! ... without will, without desire and without work!
There you are! (Still fussing with his ashes, puffing and drawing
in with his mouth — — drawing in and puffing.)

D u m   M a r i n (whose eyes are fixed upon the struggle with the ex-
tinguished tobacco, somewhat important but without expression):
Something must have clogged it!

M a s t e r   L u k s h a (mumbling as above):
Its soul be clogged! (He draws, draws and behold! — Blue
smoke rises beneath the kindled ashes and slowly, straightlined
it soars into the quiet air as if the bees of Mato Krila in Giman
were burning. One little boat quietly cuts the guilded bay into
which the darkhaired Petka is gazing): Here .... here ....

D u m   M a r i n (sighing as if the were tired, too):   ·
Bravo, yes!

M a s t e r   L u k s h a (throwing a mouthful of smoke into the pure, blue
air, is reciting a verse as if recalling something):
"And to heaven returns what from heaven came!" (To
Dum Marin): Where is that from? ....

D u m   M a r i n (surprised, angry, raising his hands towards heaven):
Where from? And still he is asking me?! ... And who
said that (reciting with pathos and rising from his chair):
In vain heavy smoke is rising from the altar,
Up to deaf heavens, mocking "raja"[1] poor!

M a s t e r   L u k s h a (waving his hand indifferently, disdainfully):
Enough! .... enough! .... you will frighten my pigeons! ....

D u m   M a r i n (collapses in his chair, as if he had not been squel-
ched, pressing his hands to his mouth he whines away in a low
voice like whispering in confession):
And this man was a poet, a statesman and he defended
us before the emperor, each of his verses kindled like
embers — — and the whole nation wanted to soar after
him, then ....

M a s t e r   L u k s h a (smoking quietly):
..... did not soar! — —

---

[1] Raja = slaves.

Dum Marin (quickly towards him):
  And who is to be blamed? Who? — — Who? ...

Master Luksha (as above):
  I.

Dum Marin (remains his mouth wide open and in his surprise nothing but a long, amazed sound comes forth):
  Oh! ...

Master Luksha (as above, quietly, naturally, now looking at the smoke now at the embers):
  Bravo! ... Thus I like you! "Oh!" and nothing more. And even if you wanted it, my dear Dum Marin, nothing else would occur to you! For not even a hundred or a thousand of "Oh" will explain to you why the noblemen without power were left like trees without veins, and why the nation without nobility was left like a body without a soul.

Dum Marin (kicking like a devil fish on a hook):
  And who tells you, Master, it is so?

Master Luksha (turning quickly around and slamming the little table with his hands, he looks sharply into his face):
  And who tells you, priest, it is not so?

Dum Marin (drawing back into his house like a snail, with a pale, frightened look):
  I am not saying anything — anything!

Master Luksha (turning again and covering the embers):
  It is better so! (Puffing two or three good whiffs.) We . . . . we of the old nobility we knew, my dear Dum Marin, how to command others and how to obey laws, cioè[1]: ourselves for we alone were power and we with the people: Liberty.

Dum Marin (mumbles, his gaze fixed upon the sheet of paper he has been scribbling upon and peevishly repeating the last sentence):
  Dunque we stopped: without will, without desires and ...

Master Luksha (emphatically):
  And "without work" (as if changing his mind about something

---

[1] What is.

he laughs shaking his head, in a very animated way). Ha, ha,
ha! Did you ever hear this new kind of mob pronouncing with
their mouth full "constitution", "parliament" .... "rights",
now they have invented frames"[1]. (Laughing uproariously.) Ha!
ha!.. all this we called in former times: fetters! ha! ha!
(Choking from cough and laughter he waves his hand scornfully
as if chasing an invisible mob. Suddenly he stops absorbed in
thoughts for new ideas befall him. Dum Marin understands, he
takes his pen and gets ready to write): And you may say
besides, Dum Marine[2], that the noblemen died because
slavery sucked out the little bit of heart they still had ...
(Drawing twice from his pipe.)

Dum Marin (involuntarily as if afraid of what is ahead of him):
Master Luksha!

Master Luksha (has overheard him, continues looking straight
ahead severely while tapping the little table with his hand):
.... For when the old, beautiful, warm delight of ruling
ceased, we should have turned up our sleeves and bent
down to it.

Dum Marin (writing in a hurry):
Slowly .... slowly! ... "and bent down to" ... (looking in
astonishment at him): To where, Master Luksha?

Master Luksha (watching quietly the smoke out of the pipe):
To the earth.

Dum Marin (his mouth distorted, he writes repeating the words
as if not understanding them):
To the earth?!

Master Luksha (half turning to him, half joking half mocking):
You don't like it, ... do you, Dum Marine? ..... Ah! .....

Dum Marin (impudently):
What are you asking me for, Master, when you already
know I don't understand you.

---

[1] Frames: a word out of the program of the Starchevich party. This very program
requested a union of all Croatian territory. Among those belonging to the party a violent
dispute arose to whether the territory should be united in the frame of the Habsburg
Monarchy or outside this frame.
[2] Dum Marine vocativ of Dum Marin.

M a s t e r L u k s h a (sinking into his chair he puts down his pipe again):

Sometimes you have reason for it, my dear Dum Marine! Write, write my bitter thoughts even if they appear strange and confused to you. (Leaning his head upon his hand): We should repent before death! (With a sad smile.) How much you ought to laugh to yourself, Dum Marine, at this old nobleman who judges others and alone he has grown old in doing nothing. (Shaking his head.) All around us changes, all perishes and grows again, woods cover abysses, new men plant new thoughts and we all do not understand it — — — just as you, Dum Marine, do not understand me. (Startling.) And yet I said all I could. I did my duty, (rising as in anger) what I knew I told. Why then was all this in vain, why did we perish and why does the idea of liberty die with us?

M a s t e r N i k o (coming in from the right, guant, tall, his face thin, his beard long and partly grey, his eyes dreamy, his shoulders drooping. He has a straw hat on his head. Walking stiffly, straight like in a dream to the chapel he gazes for a minute at the font and pats it with his long thin fingers. Then again, with the same quiet steps he goes to the background and there he remains like a picture watching the cypresses of Saint Michael).

D u m M a r i n (writing, writing, but just the same like every day he looks at him sideways and like every day he mumbles):

At your service, Master Niko!

M a s t e r L u k s h a (he has seen everything, some far off goodnatured smile flits across his glowering face. Shaking his head and closing his eyes for an instant he puts his hands on Dum Marin's shoulder continuing quietly but emphatically):

Add this before the ringing of Ave Maria, Dum Marine: "When we buried power, we should have bowed to the soil, — — — the soil which we had been enslaving and, glory-fying for ourselves during thousands of years, we should have loved it for its own sake as we love the living body of our mother or our wife, with much blood and much compassion." (A pause. In the garden a little bell is heard and also the voice of a little girl asking): Who is it?

D u m   M a r i n (writing):
..... compassion."

M a s t e r   N i k o (as above in a drawling, dry tone):
And where is „Lorko" [1]?

M a s t e r   L u k s h a (coldly, simply, not turning around):
They threw him away, Niko.

M a s t e r   N i k o (returning again the same way, his lips making a noise involuntarily):
He will return!..... He!..... he! He will return! (Patting the font again and passing Luksha, in the same voice, without stopping nor looking at him):
I am going!

M a s t e r   L u k s h a (bending his head and gazing at the stone):
Where are you going?

M a s t e r   N i k o (as above, close to the door):
To Africa (goes).

M a s t e r   L u k s h a (sighing he throws himself lazily upon a chair):
Well, where did we stop, Dum Marine.

D u m   M a r i n (reading):
"With much compassion."

M a s t e r   L u k s h a (going on talking, looking at the calm sky):
..... "If we had been as great as Nikolica, Marojica and Pracat[2] and the rest of our sea-fearing men and nobility, while enslaved we should have tried to keep the soul of our nation, the soul we had planted on these rocks."

D u m   M a r i n (writing, he is delighted):
Sublime idea! .... (Again a little bell is heard in the garden.)

---

[1] Lorko an oldfashioned beautiful villa of the dukes of Guchetich in Grush in pure rennaissance of the 16th century which was pulled down twenty years ago by one of our "Americans"* who had a modern villa built in the same place (villa Elisa). Lorko from Italian: l'orco = devil, thus the people named the destroyed villa saying that ghosts were keeping sentinel in it.

[2] Nikolica, Marojica and Pracat, three of the most famous dukes and heroes of Dubrovnik.

* American, a man usually a peasant who has made money in America and then returned a rich gentleman.

Master Luksha (flaring up):
Again the doors are closed! All right! Well, I am not stirring. (To Dum Marin.) Then say: "And instead of this we gave ourselves to the highest bidder".

Dum Marin (exited, would like to rise):
Ah! .... but this is too much ...

Master Luksha (rises, forcing, him back with his firm fists, talking as if hammering it in):
And let it stand black on white that while in liberty we shut up our daughters in convents to fade and curse virginity, and we could have married them with rich men of the people and thus purified their blood, it was our duty while in slavery to take into our empty, barren palaces the bastards we had been sowing upon the rocks of Konavlje.

Dum Marin (who has been wriggling like a fish on a hook until now has stopped his ears, he is puffing from fear and shame, finally he suceeds in freeing himself out of Luksha's fist, he jumps up, throws away his pen and runs out like mad):
I don't want to! ... I don't want to! ... But, Master Luksha! But what are you talking about?! How are you not ashamed?!

Master Luksha (sitting in his chair he is convulsed with laughter):
Ha, ha, ha! ... No! ... No! ... I am not ashamed, Dum Marine, no! (Getting up, still laughing soothes him in a friendly way): It is true! It was a sin ... but did you see what kind of young people grew out of it? What fists! What chests! What foreheads! ...

Dum Marin (still looking frightened at him):
And you would plant them, Master, in these castles?! ...

Master Luksha (letting him go scornfully):
Well, who knows? (Walking up and down).

Dum Marin (folding his hands, peeping tranquilly at him behind his glasses):
If your late father should hear you! ...

Master Luksha (stopping, scowling and sharply):
My noble father is sleeping at Saint Michael's [1] and very soon we three shall be there, too, and then one more beautiful stone from our walls will fall into the depth. Thus the noblemen willed it! .. (With bitter irony, motionless.) We don't want to give slaves to a foreign master. Ha, ha! Great nobility! ... and meanwhile our city remained without a soul ...

Dum Marin (shaking his head he picks up the papers from the little table):
.... and forgets.

Master Luksha (sits, his head buried in his hands):
And this is our punishment! (Shaking, he gets up in a sort of usual voice quickly): Well, here you are! ... it's all your fault, Dum Marine, your.

Dum Marin: Mine?! ....

Master Luksha (nervously half joking):
Why do you ask? Why do you draw out my thoughts which are sleeping more deeply than the noblemen on Saint Michael's?
(The girl Vica comes in with a few letters.)

Vica (handing them over to him):
The letter-carrier brought them.

Master Luksha (opening them):
I have told you about a hundred times that the doors are to be open at dinner time. Every day the same annoyance, the same bells.

Vica: What do you expect, Master! ...

Master Luksha: There is a regiment of you! One is to stand in the court and receive ..... (Vica goes. Smiling to Dum Marin and pointing to the open letters.) How some words quiet the nerves! Here! .... this is a summons to pay my taxes, ... and this a "proclamation" one for Pero and the other one for Fran. Tomorrow are communal elections .... Ha!

[1] Cemetery.

Dum Marin (behind his glasses):
Whom are you voting for, Master Luksha? . . .

Master Luksha (tearing up the letters and throwing them down the parapet):
For nobody.

Dum Marin (who has been looking down from the terrace):
And intanto[1] here is your wine from Konavlje, Master Luksha. Almeno[2] here there are no parties.

Master Luksha (frowning haughtily):
Annoyances! . . Now I'll have to listen to them, receive them, and Stijepo has gone to Cavtat about the wheat . . . U!! . . . .

Vica (coming from the garden):
They are asking, Master, who will receive the new wine?

Master Luksha (as above):
What do I care! Tell whomever you like it. (Vica goes.)

Dum Marin (taking his hat from the chair):
And now: at your service![3] (Pointing to the chapel.) I'll pray an Ave Maria in there. I have a long way home.

Master Luksha (walking upon the terrace):
Say one more, so that God may enlighten your mind.

Dum Marin (near the chapel):
And for you, too, Master Luksha, so you won't speak any more such things!

Master Luksha (laughing):
And you have not yet heard half of it!

Vuko (comes in from the garden. Wearing summer cloth the way they do in Konavlje. He is holding a straw hat in his hand, tall, broad shouldered, of a beautiful manly profile, with deep green eyes, a thick brown moustache covering his big sensuous mouth

---

[1] Meanwhile.
[2] At least.
[3] In the original he mocks the new fashion of saluting, saying: "auntie, your servant!" Allusion to the greeting "servus" (≈ your slave) brought to Dubrovnik by German officers, so people making fun of them said they went so far as to say: auntie, your servant.

and sparkling teeth. His hands are large and sinewy. He is all aglow from the heat of the sun. Stopping at the entry he salutes quietly lifting his hand to his forehead):
Good evening, Master!

Master Luksha (walking as above):
What is it?

Vuko (as above):
I brought you three cart loads of new wine, each of 60 barrels. Here is an account of it, Master, from your manager in Gruda. (He hands him a letter.)

Master Luksha (taking the letter and looking it over):
Very well. But why didn't you come earlier? It will soon grow dark and Stijepo is not here, either......

Vuko (who has been wiping the perspiration of his face and putting back into his belt his red handkerchief trimmed with yellow flowers):
I know, Master. But you see the gendarmes at Dupac detained us. (Spitting upon the terrace.) They were as hard as a stone and fussing around and looking everything over as if we were coming from the Turkish Krajina.

Master Luksha (mumbling below his moustache):
They would take out one's soul!

Vuko: Don't worry, Master, about the new wine. I told Vica to open the store-house. And I'll pull in the casks.

Master Luksha (looking at him):
How will you do it, you alone?

Vuko (looking at his hands, frankly almost merrily):
I am young, and thanks God and the Holy Trinity, I am strong.

Master Luksha (gazing for an instance at this heroic youthfulness):
Well, do as you know best.

Vica (coming in from the chamber, peevishly):
I have opened the store-house for you, Vuko. If you need anybody else, I shall call in a porter to help you take in the carts.

Vuko (as above):
What shall I do with a porter!

Dum Marin (leaving the chapel and wanting to pass quickly).

Master Luksha: Wait for me, Dum Marine, I'll accompany
you . . . . .

Vuko (somewhat embarrassed to Master Luksha twisting his hat
between his fingers):
If you permit me, Master, I should have something to tell you.

Master Luksha:
When there will be a chance (handing his pipe to Vica).
Here — take it — and bring my hat and my cane. —
And don't forget to give him a good supper.

Vica (ill-humoured):
Like everybody else.

Master Luksha (somewhat angrily and scornfully):
Naturally, you won't give him pan di Spagna[1]. What is for
service is good for him. And put a white pillow under
his head tonight. (Vica goes to the next room.)

Vuko (saluting with his hand):
Well then, adio Master. (He turns walking slowly out into the
garden.)

Master Luksha (still gazing after him):
Adio! Shut the store-house when you leave it.

Vuko (descending):
Don't worry, Master. (He goes.)

Vica (carrying hat and cane out of the room, peevishly):
Here they are, Master . . . . .

Master Luksha (putting the hat on his head and taking the cane):
And pray, what are you grumbling about?

Vica (ill-natured):
I am saying that Vuko should have stayed at home instead
of sneaking around here again.

---

[1] Pan di Spagna = a sweet cake the Sisters of the Churches used to make.

Master Luksha: Sneaking around? — —

Vica (as above):

Certainly. It is about a month ago since you said you would not give him Jela Konavoka for a wife. —

Master Luksha (surprised):

Him?

Vica: Didn't you tell his father you would not give her to him, Master?

Master Luksha: What about it? — He brought the wine and tomorrow he is going away.....

Vica (angrily):

It is easy enough for you, Master. But who will toil for Jela, wash, take care of the sheep? For a month she has been weeping and dreaming about that „belleza"[1] and her work does not get done.

Master Luksha (striking the ground with his cane):

Well, what then..... — Let her weep, let her dream. She will stay — and Vuko will go away without her.

Dum Marin: And why don't you give her to him?

Vica: Look here, I have been talking to Master, too, Dum Marine?

Master Luksha (cross but laughing):

Bravo, yes. Here is a nice duet. Because, — perchè I don't want to (explaining himself). Ma sapete[2]. I can't command my own servants any more. — Yes, of course — constitution, parliament. (Turning to Vica.) Send her to the neighbourhood tonight to spin wool. Thus she won't see him........

Dum Marin (slowly going away with Luksha): "Romeo e Giullietta"?

Master Luksha (striking his cane): And I to play the part of "D. Bartolo". (To Dum Marin). Del resto[3] they would make a nice couple.

---

[1] Beauty.
[2] But you know!
[3] Besides.

Dum Marin (slowly to Master Luksha):
Alas! Our people! If there were a thousand such men with your head, Master Luksha, we should be free. (They descend into the garden.)

Vica (to Master Luksha):
If anybody comes what shall I say?

Master Luksha: There is the terrace and there is Madam Mare. (Goes away.)

Vica (along the terrace):
And if madam Slave should come?

The voice of Master Luksha: Ha! Ha! — with her armata[1]! When I don't see her — she may. Ha! Ha! — (His laughter is heard from the garden.)

Vica (remains on the top of the steps, saluting):
Take care going down the steps, Master! At your service, Dum Marin!

The voice of Dum Marin: Adio, Vica!

Vica (looking for an instant after them she returns to the terrace. She is angry and out of sorts. Starting to clear up the table):
Adio, — adio and may the lord enlighten you! (Straightening out the disorder.) They all speak and cry all afternoon: Vica, Coffee! Jele, the pipe! Pere, the cane! — ah! — (Picking up all the papers.) All papers! — (Opening a box she stuffs everything into it.) Here: It would only want to have the wind blow them away as it happened some time ago! — I should have to sweep them — by no means! (Closing the box. Ma gia![2] Arranging chairs.) They are all the same. The lord forgive me! — — — all crazy.

Master Niko (coming in from the right. Dressed as before carrying in his hand a valise and an overcoat. — Going again to the chapel he is mumbling on his way to Vica without looking at her in a dry, sharp voice):
Vica! — — — bauo[3]!

---

[1] army.
[2] Well then.
[3] The trunk.

Vica (stopping in surprise and looking glowingly at him):
What — are you going away, Master Niko?.........

Master Niko (coming to the font and gazing at it, patting it, and in the same automatic step he goes to the back of the terrace, as above):
The steamer leaves at 7. — — — Dunque. Did you understand?

Vica (shaking, still more angry):
Yes, yes — subito ... I'll send you Ilija down to the molo. — Is there anything else?

Master Niko (looking off into the distance without turning):
You are still here .....

Vica (running):
Here I am, — here. (To herself.) Almeno [1] one less. (Catching sight of the shadow of Madam Mare appearing at the door of the room.) Here is another one. — — — Yes? By no means ..... I'll across the garden. — — — (Quickly descending the stairs.)

Madam Mare (tall, thin appears at the door on the right. Holding on to the threshold with both her hands. She is blind. Her face is old, faded, but full of traces of former beauty. Her hair, almost entirely grey is held back tight and parted into two locks down to her ears. She wears a black cap upon her head. Dressed in a grey gown a black woolen shawl thrown across her shoulder. Her eyes are big, expressionless, empty. She comes slowly but surely upon the terrace. Stopping a minute, she remains motionless as if listening, then she calls):
Vica! — — — Vica! — — — where are you?

Master Niko (without moving or turning):
She is not here.

Madam Mare (surprised and joyfully):
Oh! You are here, Niko.(Slowly going up to the little table and touching everything that has been placed on the same spot for ages. She sits down in a chair. Quietly and gently.) It semed to me I heard her voice.

---

[1] At least.

Master Niko (as above):
She went to find me a prentice.

Madam Mare (taking a stocking out of her pocket and wanting to knit, raising her head):
Oh? — — —

Master Niko (coming down to the little table, dreamy, indifferent, void of feeling, as before, in the same cruel, dry tone):
Adio Mare.

Madam Mare (turning toward his voice as if looking at him):
Where are you going?

Master Niko (going slowly back where he came from):
I don't care.

Madam Mare (sighing and shaking her head, her hands dropping to her side):
As always. — —

Master Niko (stopping at the entry):
Dunque — — — at your service! — — —

Madam Mare (rising, quiet, but as if her voice and hands were trembling a little):
Niko, — — — forgive, but you know (with an embarrassed smile) how silly I am. Ever since you have been roaming around the world I always felt worried — but never so much — as today.

Master Niko (involuntarily coming towards her, it is evident something is troubling him infinitely):
Foolish. — — —

Madam Mare (coming up to him as before):
I said so, too. But what do you want? — We are old — (In a lower tone.) Older every year. — (Putting one hand on his shoulder.) Can't you stay?

Master Niko (shaking his head and closing his eyes. In a hard voice):
No. —

Madam Mare (as above, thoughtfully):
It must be because Grush is Grush no more.

Master Niko (with restrained, scornful laughter):
They have thrown away Lorko.

Madam Mare (troubled in a lower voice, nearer):
They have filled up the ocean below the wharf ..

Master Niko (hard, far off):
They have cut through Nunciata . . . .

Madam Mare (still lower):
Did you hear it this morning? — — — (As if frightened.)
— It whistled. — — —

Master Niko (in a voice like dry branches whistling in the wind):
He! — he! — ferata[1].

Madam Mare (going away from him she slowly approaches the chapel):
Well, you see, it came, too. (As if in great pain contracting her shoulders.) Go, — go. — There everything is new and you forget — and here? All is old and hurting you. (Stopping and turning toward him. Lovingly.) Ah, — if they could hear us, Niko. — They would laugh at us.

Master Niko (taking again his valise and overcoat, without feeling):
He! He! — Soon they won't do even that. (Going away.) Adio Mare! — (Goes without looking at her.)

Madam Mare (remaining alone as if rooted to the same spot):
Adio, Niko. — Take care of yourself. (Listening to his distant steps.) Something is hurting him. (Passing with her hand over her forehead.) I still see him. — — — How handsome and gay he was! — (Thoughtfully.) I never asked anybody: Whether he has grown grey (going towards the background, sighing), he, too obeyed our father. — Alone! — alone! (A pause. She has come to the middle of the terrace. All the sunset glow of sky and sea and the gorgeous view of that green paradise from Montevjerno to Ston have engulfed the lonely, sad, grey apparition of a blind woman. She sighs deeply.) Ah! — — — How sweetly Petka[2] smells. — If I could only see it. —

---

[1] Train.
[2] A mountain.

The voice of Vuko (from the road):
Hallo, young man! — Open the store-house for me! ...

Madam Mare (bending her head in a distant voice):
I don't understand.

Vica (coming in):
Here she is. — Ma brava. — How she walks around.

Madam Mare (as above):
Where did Master Luksha go?

Vica (escorting her up to the table):
He is walking with Master Dum Marin. (Madam Mare sits down finding her stocking again.) Ah! do you know, Madame Mare, he who is wanting Jela, has come again.

Madam Mare (full of care):
Take care of her, you know! I don't want any kind of silliness! — and what's he like?

Vica (scornfully):
Like everybody else from Konavlje!

Madam Mare (smiling):
And what are you? — A princess? — Ah?! I like that! (At the gate Ida appears holding an immense bouquet of mountain flowers and a little bag in her hand. She slowly sneaks up putting a finger upon her lips so that Vica should not speak.)

Vica (catching sight of her would like to speak — but mustn't, then merrily):
Oh! — — —

Madam Mare (knitting her stocking):
What's the matter with you?

Ida (simply dressed in a grey skirt fashionably cut and white batiste waist with black dots, a dark blue tie under the English collar. A straw "canotier" on her head. Under it appears a youthful, pale, fine face with big blue eyes. Her brown hair is gathered up in the back. She is tall. Her movements are simple, graceful. She quickly approaches behind Madam Mare and handing her with one hand a bouquet of heather she stops close behind her.)

Changing a little her voice and imitating an old childish game of Dubrovnik, she whispers):
"Cu — cu — cu!"

Madam Mare (drawing a deep whiff from the flowers):
Ah! — — — (Turning her head towards the voice and smiling an old-fashioned amiable smile she keeps up the fun): — —
Where are you standing?

Ida (as above):
On the terrace.

Madam Mare (as above):
"Whom do you have?"

Ida (as above):
A wicked aunt who does not love me! — — —

Madam Mare (joyfully):
Ida! — — (Drawing her nearer and embracing her,)

Ida (kneeling beside her she holds the bouquet of flowers up to her face):
And this?

Madam Mare (smelling, them and raising her head as if following a far off call):
This? — This is the heather growing on the stones! — (Turning to Ida somehow full of longing): It has blossomed, has it?

Ida (rising she takes off her "canotier" and sits down upon the little chair near her):
It has covered the whole mountain, auntie, "like God's blessing"!

Madam Mare (caressing the flowers):
How beautifully you speak today!

Ida: That's exactly what a poor woman said to me this morning at the gates of our Lady of Mercy.

Madam Mare (as if to herself):
Poverty is a rock, too, — and how it blossoms!

Ida (taking out one flower from the bouquet):
I should bet you don't know what this is!

M a d a m   M a r e (touching and smelling the little yellow calix of the flower):
Strange! — It smells like earth after rain . . . . . (Startling suddenly almost rising towards Ida. Her voice full of infinite delight and remembrances): — My cyclamens! — — —

I d a (leaning her head upon Madam Mare's chair, telling slowly, naively, with an accent as if relating old tales to a child):
Alas! You see. they, too, have started on their way, and there are so many of them! They begin at our Lady's and they go, always one following the other, one — and when they get tired they rest below the milestone in the shade of big olive-trees and here they whisper softly from flower to flower the word[1] which they must never forget on their way, and they light their tiny little lamps. (Bending close to Madam Mare's face.) Yes, Yes! — Thus yellow, tiny, stuck into the black earth — and quiet like candles upon the altar, they seem from ta distance like candles on "Corpus Dei".(A little thoughtful looking far away, almost to herself.) They, too, know where they are going! . . . . .

M a d a m   M a r e (all lost in her voice):
To Saint Michael's — don't they?

I d a (staring at the little flower):
Yes, auntie! — and do you know whom they are escorting? (Smiling sadly.) The dead body! — —

M a d a m   M a r e (almost gaily, leaning face to face):
Ah! — — Don't you think daughter, how nicely they will light us up when we rest upon Lapad. (Straightening up almost majestically.) Oh! How I shall exclaim under my stone: "Finalmente"[2], we are among our own people!

I d a (she, too rises, grasping her hand and walking slowly in front of the terrace, with purpose):
A intanto!

M a d a m   M a r e (patting her hand):
Oh bella! We have to live, — we have to work.

---

[1] Praised be our Lord.
[2] Finally.

I d a (lively, piercingly, as if the gates out of which her suppressed longing was rushing forth, had opened, — stopping and pressing closely to her aunt):

Yes, — — yes! What a beautiful sane word it is: work! Don't you feel your soul getting brighter, when you hear it, auntie? — No, you don't know what joy it is to say: "I am earning for myself and my dear people and — finalmente — I am free!"

M a d a m M a r e (who has been attentively listening to the sound of this joyful exclamation somewhat surprised):

Here, behold . . . . . her "enthusiasm"!

I d a (as above, holding the old woman round her waist, leaning face to face):

And to save a fiorin every month — — one by one — — as the ants are doing before winter. And when the wind begins to blow to buy something for mother that will keep her warm, to send something to brother in Vienna so that he, too, poor man might have a little ease!? . . . . .

M a d a m M a r e (going a little away from her, agitated, glowering):

What are you dreaming about?

I d a (putting her hands upon her heart so as to appease its beating, even more piercing, pale in her face):

If I should tell you auntie, I am going to America . . . . .

M a d a m M a r e (shaking her head):

That's not for you! — No, no . . . .

I d a (exclaiming):

Ah! how well you know me. . . . . . And — how would it be if I read something to you? (Running to the little wall where she had left her bag, quickly taking out a letter.)

M a d a m M a r e (sitting down in the chair, mumbling):

There is something in your voice . . . . . hm! I don't understand . . (Sadly to herself.) As if she were going away, too! — (Smelling the heather which is on the little table.)

I d a: Now you will hear! — — — But listen well . . . . . (Reading in a strong school accent.) "The Imperial, County School Committee."

Madam Mare (frowning):
What is that?! — — —

Ida (laughing):
It is not in our language — but you will understand,
Dunque .... has decided to appoint Miss Ida Countess
Luccari-Volzo (she has grown pale but with a smile on her
face she is watching the old lady's face) — temporary assistant
teacher! —

Madam Mare (rising, scowling, excited):
And this means to say? — — —

Ida (throwing the letter upon the little table and pressing close to
her, in an animated, moved, quick tone):
It means to say when the house is empty and mother old,
and when one does not wish to sell oneself for money
neither to a peasant nor to a rich man, — neither to a
foreigner, one must do what you, auntie, said: one must
work, turn into a schoolmaam. —

Madam Mare (retreating and trembling, getting hold of the chair
she sinks into it as if disappearing in its depth):
A schoolmaam! — you?! The granddaughter of Orsat the
Great!

Ida (pale, but firm like the slabs on the terrace, leaning on both
her hands upon the little table. In her voice there is a great
soundless calm):
Say piutosto[1]: the daughter of Vlagj Luccari-Volzo who
died somewhere at a hospital in Constantinople, a vladika[2]
of Dubrovnik, an Austrian countess without house nor
yard etc. — And now a temporary assistant teacher in
Pila with a yearly salary as it says in the appointment —
of 350 fiorins ... — ha! ha!

Madam Mare (as above, lost among invisible things):
I see the voices of all those, there, as well as you see
the living people. Even now while I listen to you I seemed
to see the nun, our relative — — — Oh! .... I was a

---

[1] Rather.
[2] Ruler.

child, — when they took me to The Three Churches — — —
yes! — yes! — You have the voice of Maria Paola. —

I d a (coming nearer):
And what did she do?

M a d a m M a r e (getting back to herself and getting hold of Ida's
head she quietly kisses her):
The same you have done and she did well.

I d a (embracing her ardently, with a deep sigh):
Ah! — auntie, if you knew! — I, too shall, be a rock now
with a few heather blossoms. (Putting on her hat she takes
the bag in which she places the letter from the little table.)
Ah! — and now quickly! — to tell mother of my good
fortune! (Charmingly.) If you knew! ... I bought a little
supper for her — but what a fine one! It will be a real
feast ...

M a d a m M a r e (sadly):
How merry you are! — — —

I d a (pulling on her gloves, gaily):
Why not! — — — believe me, auntie, this is the blessing
of my poor woman.....

M a d a m M a r e (in a plaintive voice as above):
And that's why you came?! (Getting up and catching on to
Ida.) Why didn't you tell me anything about it before —
who knows! — we might have. — —

I d a (charmingly, carressing her white locks):
Auntie! — Auntie! — and why are we still the last
"vladika"? (Slowly, half jokingly but her tears choking her throat.)
Just imagine — 350 fiorins a year! (In a lower tone.) A few
tears less — and sometimes a little more soup! — (More
cheerfully.) You don't say anything, to have children de-
pending on you. — Many, many little children of our
own nation and that foreign people do not pull out what
Dundo[1] Luksha calls "the soul which we have planted
there", and try hard to plant a few of your yellow flowers —
so that they might always smell of our soil. — — —

---

[1] Uncle.

Madam Mare (stepping a little foward all entranced by the tone of the voice, and passing over her face with her hand as if listening to a far off roaring, quietly as if to herself):
Always the same! — Martyrs — keepers. —

Ida (looking at her in surprise and fear):
What are you pondering about, auntie?

Madam Mare (getting back to herself and carressing her):
Don't forget me now. Madam Schoolmaam!

Ida (embracing her):
You?! — You! — for all the good you have done me now! — Ah! How afraid I was of my aunt Mare! — Ha! ha! But you will see me now! Vladika! — from head to heel! Ha! ha! (From below the terrace out on the ocean snatches of music and exclamations are heard.)

Madam Mare (amazed):
Who is it?

Ida (running to the bottom):
Ah! — (Looking down.) If you saw them. (Hastily running to her.) Slave et Compagnie! They certainly had somekind of a great spree with the foreigners from the Hotel and the officials di terra e di mare[1]. — — —

Madam Mare (agitated):
The Lord deliver us! Let Vica receive them ... They can have the terrace and the garden and fool around as much as they want to. I shall intanto[2] lock myself up in the chapel. I have my rosaries to pray anyway ....

Vica (running up the stairs from the garden all out of breath, angrily):
Well, what did I tell you?! — — — mere "foreigners"! ...

Madam Mare (smiling):
Vica mine, amuse yourself! — In the empty house they are masters (opening the doors of the chapel) — and in the chapel mistress am I! —

---

[1] From land and sea.
[2] Meanwhile.

I d a (looking down the parapet):

All! — Au complet!? ha! ha! — Ché típi!¹ (quickly kissing Madam Mare). Here are those, auntie, who have forgotten everything. Therefore (bowing laughingly to the one and to the other). Adio — and scoot! (Leaves running away trough the chamber.)

M a d a m   M a r e (on the threshold of the chapel smiling):

Vica mine! — Adio — and scoot (slamming the door she turns the key on the inside. The squeaking of the lock is heard.)

V i c a (looking on in anger and in surprise at the one and the other one):

And I — with — them? (The music and din are coming nearer.) Why not!..... Bonasera — — — and scoot — — — (Running out through the door on the right. The stage remains empty, the sun hides.)

B a r o n e s s L i d i a (29 years old, tall, her hair dark and thick, her eyes big and grey, her lips are too red, her waist too small. She wears an elegant summer tennis-suit. She walks in big rythmical steps. The rustling of silk petticoats accompanies her. On her head she has a straw "canotier" trimmed with a narrow black ribbon. She is the type of a modern lady. When she laughs, and she does so very often, her brilliant white teeth illumunate her whole face with a kind of sensuous, defiant reflection. Jumping in swiftly from the garden she starts running across the terrace and stops motionless in the middle. Taking in this loneliness with a surprised far reaching look she shivers. But she does so only for a moment for immediately exclaiming merrily, she runs to the parapet on the right and clapping her hands she calls to those who are below):

Hurrah! nobody! — — (She is about to turn around and finds herself close to a person who has slowly sneaked up after her from the garden. This is).

C o u n t H a n s O e t t i n g s h e i m (tall, lean, he might be 34 years old. His hair closely cut he has a fine profile, sleepy eyes, a reddish moustache. Through the tastly white English tennis-suit the harmonious movements of the sinewy trained body are visible. Like a tiger he has crawled up after her, his face resembling one, and when she turns around he catches hold of both her hands, wedging her close to himself. Body to body, breath to breath he

¹ What types.

wants to kiss her burning lips, and when she cries out from fear and surprise, he whispers, sensuously, boldly):
"Endlich allein."

Baroness Lidia (defending herself quietly, her eyes flashing, a smile on her face):
No — not here! — What kind of manners are those! — But Hans — Hans.....

Count Hans (as above, passionately almost brutally):
Here or elsewhere, c'est égal! — but for three days I have not seen you — do you understand! — — Three kisses! — — — Neither less nor more.....

Baroness Lidia (laughing as above):
If my husband should come?.....

Count Hans (as above, laughing):
You sent him to take care of the sandwiches in the boat..... (in a lower tone sensuously). What do you think I am here for in your Oriental nest where everything is old and dead for the love of the Hotel Imperial and you don't see I am only living for you — the only flower on these barbarian rocks.

Baroness Lidia (laughing in a loud and uproarious way, swiftly catches hold of his head with both her hands, kissing him upon his mouth):
Shut up, Teuton! Here! when you want it! — — This one is for me.....

Count Hans (pressing her close to him as a snake to a tree):
And this one for me (kissing her).

Baroness Lidia (releasing herself and beating him with her red parasol):
And this one for him! — — — Ha! ha! ha!

Voices from below:
Lidia!..... Lidia!..... What are you doing..... where are you?! — —

Baroness Lidia (dragging count Hans to the parapet):
Let us mock them a little! — — (bowing with him to the

people who are clapping their hands, crying, cheering). Thanks!
thanks! — — — a nice couple, aren't we?..... Ha! ha!
Come up. — An ideal terrace! — We can rehearse once
more our operette..... —

Voices from below:
Bravo! — — — bravo! — — —

Count Hans (speaking down from the terrace):
Let the musicians come up first and you place yourselves
"en position" for the "chorus of the Rogues" — — and
here I am.....

Baroness Lidia (clapping her hands with joy):
Ah! — Superbe! — — Wait — a minute — let us fix the
stage.....

Count Hans (running up to the little table and skillfully carrying
it in an instant as well as the table and chairs into the corner
between the house and the chapel. Everything now is quick, without a pause):
Here — ready —

Baroness Lidia (helping him hurriedly):
Voilà! — and now Monsieur le voleur — forward, march!

Count Hans (trying to catch her):
Look out! You still owe me one! — — (Three musicians
are coming in from the garden, the violin, the. flute and the
zither.)

Baroness Lidia (running and catching sight of the musicians
quickly and in a low tone to him):
Keep quiet! Don't you see?! — — — (She pushes him crying):
forward, march! (and he flashing a look at her goes away running and smiling down the stairs into the garden, then she comes!
back! laughingly, but tired) Ah !..... how tiresome he is
getting! — (To the musicians who have quietly stayed near the
seat on the terrace close to the staircase on the right and who
have been watching all this as if seeing old things) And you
place yourselves here, — and strike up the chorus "della
Gran Via". Did you learn it for to-morrow?

Three Musicians (our usual, quiet artists from the city who play to everybody and who have seen all[kinds):
Altrochè[1], Madam!

Baroness Lidia! Very well. Well, then when I give you the word! (Bending down the terrace and catching sight of the hidden group below,) Herrlich! — — — Just le dernier cri! — Only keep time! — Baron, take care of the young girls! Ha! ha! ha! — — — But — attention. Only mothers are forbidden to come! — — —

Voices from below (uproarious and in laughter):
Bravo! — no! — no! — Dunque — move on! — — —

Baroness Lidia (as above):
When I clap my hands twice, then entrez! And you below — Theatergesindel — wait! ... (Rushing up to the armchair in the corner near the chapel she comfortably smiles into it.) Well then?! — (Clapping her hands.) En avant! ... (The musicians strike up "The Chorus of the Rogues" from the Spanish "Zarzuela" La Gran Via, — when behold one after one coming from the garden exactly to the rhythm of the ballet of that graceful music in the piquant position of the Spanish "Ratas" Count Hans, Emica, baron José, Jelka, Marko Tudisi and Ore. The noblemen are all dressed like Hans in fine white tennis-suits. Their stockings are visible under the turned up white trousers, their shirts and ties are in various fashionable shades. The young girls, too, are dressed as it is customary now for playing tennis, similar to baroness Lidia. Each one wears a straw canotier with narrow colored ribbon. The whole group is charming and tasteful and in each line the routine of the refined' cosmopolitan life can be traced. The music is playing and the procession dancing goes the same way to the bottom of the terrace. Here they all turn at once like a ballet quadrille descending in one column the whole breadth of the terrace towards the audience. Flexible movement of the body coquettish looks and lively understanding of the situation perfect the illusion of a real theatrical performance.)

Baroness Lidia (sitting in an armchair accompanies the whole scene like a real stage manager with facial expression, with rhythmical measure beating of her hands as well as with exclamations of satisfaction and laughter):

[1] And how well.

Bravissimi! Ha! ha! — Please Jelka lift your legs a little higher! You, too, Ore! — Nur keine Prüderien, Mesdames![1] — Thus! — Bravo! — And now — top!

(At this word the whole column which is taking in the breadth of the stage, turns around pirouetting and begins to sing "The Chorus of the Rogues" accompanied with characteristic unisonant movements of a real "café concert". The chorus is divided according to voices in three groups, each of which begins with the words):

— "Son il primo ladrone!"
— "Il secondo son io!"
— "Son il terzo!"

(Then they begin from the wellknown score. The whole chorus is executed in the elegant tone of amateur performances and when the singing ceases, the youthful procession turns right about and following the accompaniment of the music walks all around the back part of the terrace and returns to the place it started from. Just then, the music stops, the group scatters cheering uproarious and merry, filling at once the rosy west which is smiling upon the stony terrace, gilding each vase each architectural line and also the picturesque whiteness of this chattering, careless, youthful flock.

Only Petka, motionless and gloomy in the dark majesty of her overthick fir-trees, looks on speechless like the Sphinx of Keops upon those whirling, mortal, tiny ants below.)

B a r o n e s s L i d i a (remaining in her armchair while the chorus lasts, following with intense interest every motion, managing now one thing now the other, unable to resist the champagne beating in her veins any more, she, too, jumps up, placing herself at the head of the procession leading it with bold movements until she herself cries):

Halt! (Thus separating the company near the entry of the garden.)

M a d a m S l a v e, M a d a m L u k r e, M a d a m K l a r a (while the chorus was thus developing, they slowly entered from the right and watching with a kind of satisfied smile of good mothers they clap their hands the minute the performance stops crying):

B r a v i! — — bravissimi! —

B a r o n e s s L i d i a (and all her party catching sight of the ladies rush up to them with uproarious ejaculations):

---

[1] Drop your prudish manners, ladies!

Oh! — — — the mothers! — — — No! — —·— We don't
want them! — — —
(The groups have melted away. The entire terrace is brimming
over with life.)

M a d a m   S l a v e (56 years old, tall, beautiful once, now too stout,
too much rigged up in a dry, sharp voice with a kind of indifferent smile and malicious accent to Lidia):
Nobody is raising her legs as high as Lidia! — — — Ha!
— — — ha! — — —

B a r o n e s s   L i d i a (indolently in a subtle way):
A la guerre comme à la guerre! Slave![1] — Del resto. —
when it is done for the poor!

M a d a m   K l a r a (60 years old, all dressed in elegant black, partly
grey, full of "esprit"):
Of course! How much higher — the more!

B a r o n   J o s é   L a s i c h (28 years old with a little standing up mous-
tache and a strong Spanish accent):
It will be printed on the poster: „For Charitable purposes!"
Well then? — — Caramba! — (Laughter):

M a d a m   S l a v e (sitting to the left in an armchair) :
Did you get a permit from the captaincy?

M a d a m   K l a r a (sitting down, too):
Why should we when the captaincy isn't doing anything
but operettas! (Madam Lukre coming up to them sits down.
They are talking.)

C o u n t   H a n s (to the right, quietly to Lidia pretending a great indifference but there is a fire in his eyes):
· Don't tell me no! — — To-morrow or never!

B a r o n e s s   L i d i a (smiling and walking carelessly with him):
And if I should say: never? — —

M a r k o   T u d i s i (small, fairhaired of an aristocratic profile, his eyes
weary, his hands beautiful is talking to Emica and Ore walking
up and down the terrace. All three are smoking cigarettes):
In the parquet there will be sitting squadrons of archdukes
and admirals! Dunque?!

---

[1] Besides.

E m i c a (naively to Marko):

If you knew Marko how afraid I am! And mother wants me to be à la Cleo de Merode. — — She says I am resembling her!

B a r o n J o s é (approaching Emica with an impudent smile):

Oh! — — — not quite yet! — — (Laughter.)

O r e (pressing to José as if frightened):

Ah! — — — look Don José! (turning the back of her neck to him.) Something is creeping down there — — there . . . . .

B a r o n J o s é (looking döwn her neck):

In veridad! — — — Nothing!

O r e (casting a long glance upon him):

Proprio[1] nothing?! . . . . .

M a d a m S l a v e (to Lukre as above):

Well, what do you want my Lukre! — There are mummies! Dundo[2] Luksha might pass. He is worrying himself perchè he wanted something and does not any more know what he wanted. Then poor Niko and Mare! Oh! — real originals! — Del resto! — — the last great noblemen . . . . . Well, what do you want! — They don't understand the times. Now only one thing is worthwhile. "He who has money is a nobleman." Thus it is. Everything else, our ancestors, the republic e tutto il resto[3] — all these are antiquities not worth a half penny.

M a d a m L u k r e (49 years old, thin, long, always tearful, not letting the glasses go out of her hand. She observes everything and everybody):

Ah! — — — purtroppo — — — When I see that Don José! (She shivers.)

M a d a m K l a r a (maliciously, cleverly):

His grandfather was one of Benesha's peasants and he went to America. Oh! there is something of a story about the late nun Maria Paola! — — — Hm! . . . In conclusione!

---

[1] Really.
[2] Uncle.
[3] And all the rest.

She died at The Three Churches and he collected millions. And here behold his grandson per la grazia di Dio[1] and his money a baron! — Ha! — ha! — — —

O r e (coming to her mother, Madam Lukre, speaking to her in a low tone):
He searched and searched and said: nothing!

M a d a m L u k r e (in a low tone to Ore):
How foolish you are! Try again . . .

M a d a m S l a v e (slowly to Madam Klara with a malicious smile):
No! — — no! — — Emica is not for America! — — Ha! — — ha! Let Lukre gnaw him!

E m i c a (coming quickly to Madam Slave, and to her mother):
Did you see how Ore is trying to catch him?

M a d a m S l a v e (slowly):
And you are wasting your time with that foolish Marko!

B a r o n J o s é (to Jelka who had been talking and laughing with Lidia and Hans):
Try, countess, la "Frangesa" merely one verse.

J e l k a (laughing boldly into the face of Don José):
First pay your admission!

L i d i a
C o u n t H a n s ⎰ (laughing):
Brava la Frangesa!

A l l (starting to clap their hands):
La Frangesa! La Frangesa! — — —

B a r o n e s s L i d i a (coming in front of the ladies, bowing):
Mesdames sans messieurs! — The curtain rises! Nina Cavalieri is singing.

A l l (as above):
Brava la Nina!

M a r k o (calling all the young group to the right):
Come here, we are the audience of the restaurant for the refrain.

---

[1] With the grace of God.

All the younger people (except Jelka running into one cluster):
La Nina! La Nina! . . . . . .

Baroness Lidia (heading them all at the door):
"Ruhig, Gesindel!" (Great laughter.) — Music! (The music strikes up.)

Jelka (standing in the middle of the terrace in a coquettish position like a tingle tangle singer and starting to sing in a small but agreeable voice the wellknown Neapolitan song):
"Songo Frangesa
E vengo da Parige."
(And when she finishes the first verse all younger people repeat the refrain):
"Oh! oh! oh! oh!
Vi pregh è nun gridá!"
(Great laughter and clapping.)

Madam Klara (meanwhile goes to the back of the terrace, calls all the company):
Quick! — quick! — There the admiral and all his officials are passing.

All (running towards the background they stay near the parapet bowing and saluting the procession which is passing in boats below the terrace):
Hurrah! (Down below the answer: "Hurrah" is heard. The whole group remains talking and looking down the bay where the sun is slowly vanishing. All the sky is one smile, one flitting of rosecolored and green tufts. But below Saint Michael's cypresses darkness is slowly descending to the shores of Grush dragging along its violet cloak of twilight.)

Marko (coming down the terrace talking with Lidia, deeply weary):
How silly all this is! How in the midst of our noisy merriment we still hear a tiny sharp voice disturbing us! (In a lower tone.) Don't you think that in face of this sunset on this terrace something is being trampled upon and something is being desecrated? —

Baroness Lidia (looking at him in a queer way):
Yes! Just in this contrast I find my enjoyment. — And may be you yours! (Smiling intimately): What are you looking at me thus?

Marko (coolly):
I am looking at your mouth worn out by kisses.

Baroness Lidia (almost angrily):
Marko! — — —

Marko (as above):
Don't get frightened. — A stone blushes, too, but keeps quiet. —

Baroness Lidia (catching hold of his arm quickly):
Yes! yes! We go down, roll around, — first slowly, then quicker and crazier down, down into the abyss ... paf! Ha! ha!

Marko (brutally eye to eye):
You already are at the bottom!

Baroness Lidia (a wicked flash in her eye):
Just at the bottom! (Hoarsely close to him convulsively): Who sold me to old general Schmidt for his money? And who tied you to masters you hate and despise?! Who? Who?

Marko (with hardly felt irony, thrusting his hands into his pocket looking somewhat impudently at her):
We are the last noblemen! Just think how we are enjoying this unhealthy overfilled life of dissolution. (In a still lower tone, so that nobody should notice he is talking of his dead love.) Why did you leave me? —

Baroness Lidia (shrugging her shoulders a scornful line around her mouth, her gaze lost in the distance):
Why? How foolish you are! And why are you playing comedy with us upon the rocks of our ancestors? (In a lower tone). When the body is dead — it must dissolve — everything — everything — to the very bones — (breaking out into bitter laughter). Du reste . . I know what you want to tell me. Just wait a little while, and I'll leave him, too! — Ha! ha!

Count Hans (running up and placing himself intimately between them looking jokingly but restlessly now at him now at her):
Where are you? Hm?! it is smelling of something here! But of what?!

Baroness Lidia (watching him with an impudent smile):
It must be — — — of sandwiches! . . .

Count Hans }
Marko } Grand! (All three taking hands go laughingly
down the back of the terrace.)

Madam Klara (walking on the terrace in a low tone to Madam Slave):
Did you see! — Elle s'affiche!

Madam Slave (with great coolness, laughing stoutly):
Elle s'en fiche, — my dear! A dopo tutto[1] as long as she is
looking for her "amante"[2] dans la societé, she is doing well!

Ore (to José, stretching out her white arm to him):
Oh — — — Gracious me — — — something got in — — —
here! — here! — — —

Baron José (looking into her sleeve, sensuously uncovering her white skin):
Ah! — Yes! — yes — — —

Ore (all joyful):
Did you find? What is it? What?

Baron José (with comical fear, then letting Ore's hand go indifferently):
Nothing! — A little louse! —

Ore (sadly with a long look):
A little louse? — — —

Emica (running up to her mother, in a low tone):
Do you see, Ore?

Madam Slave (in a low voice):
Take him into the Garden! Don't always be as timid as a
hen. One more carnival. — And they will all call you an
old maid! — — (In the distance from Saint Michael the bell
of Ave Maria is heard — quite tiny and as if muffled by the
masses of green, while way down the "Christ" in Grush[3] answers

---

[1] After all.
[2] Lover.
[3] Pronounce sh like s in measure.

restrained like an echo. The ruddiness of the sky has faded away. Petka has grown quite black upon the golden mosaic of the setting sun. Nobody listens to the nightly greeting of the cypresses.)

B a r o n e s s L i d i a (with overwhelming gaiety to Marko so that everybody can hear her):
And now! — — — Let's go! Aux enfers![1]

A l l t h e y o u n g p e o p l e (in one exclamation):
Aux enfers! — — (A wild richness is sweeping around out of the tiny sounds of our wretched musicians, and has entered the blood, the feet and nerves of the soulles young people. Through the pious peacefulness of the sleeping castle and through praying ᴠnature the firy "galop-cancan" of Offenbach's Orfeus is whirling as a kind of ultimate challenge of the new people to the quiet dying of thousand years old ideas and generations. All the young people are dancing, keeping on like mad in one column, singing and laughing incessantly.
The mothers pretending to be horrified, laughing with a kind of inner satisfaction disappear into the room on the right. At the head of everybody Lidia, a modern bachantis, dances passionately. There is a fire in her eyes and upon her overwhite teeth. All this tempest of merriment lasts but a few minutes; the whole of life is contained in it. But suddenly the strong, inexorable tinkle-tinkle of the old chapel bell sounds upon the terrace, its rope being pulled by invisible hands. Like a mechanical game suddenly brought to a stop, the figures remaining in their dancing position, with a kind of carved doll-like smile. All the people stand speechless, motionless, as if turned to stones listening to the brass bell ringing way up there in the evening's gold.)

B a r o n e s s L i d i a (waking up first, in a kind of empty, quiet laughter she puts her finger to her mouth):
Whist! — — — the terrace is getting holy! — — — (The musicians are running down the stairs into the garden.)

C o u n t H a n s (wanting to go into the chapel):
Somebody is mocking us!

B a r o n e s s L i d i a (stopping him, piercingly):
Somebody is praying!

M a r k o (firmly, almost brutally in a low tone to Lidia):
Don't you understand this is no place for us?

---

[1] To hell.

Baroness Lidia (in a low tone to the rest):

As we came — let us go! (Placing herself at the head of all in the position of the former chorus.) Rogues! — forward march! (and again the procession forms and reechoes in quick measure but in a lower tone the "Chorus of the Rogues" then vanishes to the right with the same ballet rhythm, the same laughter, the same coquettery, the same grace, always accompanied by the chasing and mocking bell. Finally the stage remains empty. One more outburst of boisterous laughter down there, when the maddened young people leave the deserted house, one more ring, and the bell is quiet. Big stillness. Slowly the doors of the Chapel open).

Madam Mare (as if the mausoleum had thrown out its dead into the light, thus she appears upon the dusky terrace. Everything is still and calm upon the white slabs of the tired terrace. Above the sky is still blossoming and the first stars are laughing out of the greenish blue. Down from Srgj a light breeze fragrant with laurel and heather is descending. There above Petka one little cloud does not want to fade away. Madam Mare remains motionless, as if listening to the echo of the vanishing voices. Her pale face is smiling. She steps forward shaking her head):

They fled — like sparrows!

Vica (hastily, crossly, out of breath, followed by two girls who immediately begin to clear up and clean the terrace, to make everything look as in the beginning):

Oh! — — — did you hear! — goodness me! — And what was she doing in there, my poor lady.....

Madam Mare (as above):

I was praying for them — and for myself.

Vica (as above):

Yes, you are as good as a Saint! — — — (the girls are going away.) Uh! — — — and those old women! — — How! they are not ashamed! They can have the sala[1] Bachich for their dirty amusements! — — — Uh! — — —

Madam Mare (comes forward, slowly, quietly):

Have you lost your mind! have you! — — — (thoughtfully to herself.) I did not understand everything — — — but

---

[1] Sala Bachich in Dubrovnik where towards the end of the XIXth century the masked balls of the people were held.

it does not seem real pleasure to me! (To Vica) If Master
Luksha should ask you, tell him I let them. (To herself.)
I can still hear Ida's voice! — and why? (She has almost
come to the room, turning towards. Vica who is closing the chapel.)
Vica! — is there a moon tonight?

Vica Yes — there it is peeping behind Petka! — It looks
like a golden sword pin[1] upon black braids! — —

Madam Mare (as above):   •
Come! — let's go into the garden.

The voice of Vuko (from the garden):
Vica! — where are you, Vica?

Madam Mare (stops and listens satisfied to the voice:
Oh! The master! so early! — — —

Vica (going towards the parapet):
Here I am! here! — — — useless hurry — — — (Bending
and looking down). Ha! ha! — The Lord forgive — (to Madam
Mare.) It is Vuko! (Answering.) What do you want, young man:

The voice of Vuko (from below):
Did the master return?

Vica (as above):
There he is coming from Lapad — Only don't cry! — — —

The voice of Vuko (as above):
Well, what do you expect! — — — a Wolf[2] like a Wolf!

Madam Mare (who involuntarily turns to the voice. Her face
showing deep emotion. She listens and thinks):
My people are making fun of me. But for me voices are
day and night, clearness and old things — and my dead,
(She shivers.) When I hear, I see.

Vica (coming back and carefully getting hold of her arm):
Let's go, Madam Mare! — — —

Madam Mare (thoughtful but cheerful, sighing deeply):
Ah! — — —

---

[1] Sword pin = in original Croatian a golden pin shaped like a sword women used to wear in their hair.
[2] Vuko means wolf in Croatian.

Vica (humbly kissing the hand which rests upon her arm):
What is my mistress sighing for?

Madam Mare (as above):
I am seeking all the time somebody after his voice, and cannot find him. (They go.)

Master Luksha (coming in from the garden out of breath with a heavy lazy step. He is talking to somebody below):
When you put away everything — then come! — (out of sorts and tired upon the terrace.) Uf! — — — those stairs, — that age! — (Coming to the seat on the right parapet he sits down sighing deeply). Ah! Finalmente! — — — (Lifts his hat and puts it somewhere near by.) — — — I got so tired — and so cross! — Uf! just cross! — almeno¹ here I can watch what I like? And can talk to myself like old maids. But what should I do I could burst! — — — (He rises striking with his cane and pointing angrily to the chimney of the electric Central looking up there and throwing smoke there to the bottom of Batala.) No! — not even here! — wherever I turn something strikes my eyes, my nose — — — Here it is! The devil himself would not have left such a chimney beyond Saint Michael?! — — — (More and more ill-humoured, more excited in the vast nightly stillness.) There is no more Grush, no more Nunciata, no more Bonini — they threw away, dug out, cut off! Then cars, tramway, — smoke, bad smells. (Knocking his hat back to his head he wanders restlessly about the empty terrace.) Well did Mare! They took away her shore and her bathhouse — And she said: "at your service"! and went to paradise! (All more nettled, because his voice gets too boisterous in the loneliness.) And everything foreign! — — — everything new! — Prentices in carriages, dust heaps in the palace! — and political parties?! — (Bursting out with laughter and anger.) Ha! Ha! — —·— and political parties! (Pointing angrily and scornfully towards Grush.) Two bands — three flags — four females and a hundred street urchins! — But! — (Striking his cane upon the terrace.) — But! the gendarmes are keeping you safe! — he! he!

¹ At least.

— you want some pikes — so as not to kill each other!
Like the common soldiers upon Christ's grave. — Ha! Ha! —
Ben detto![1] Like common soldiers! — — — (Choked by cough
and anger he leans upon the little table till it stops. His large
body is trembling all over his face getting blue. Then breathing
heavily and scornfully waving his hand as if everything was over.)
I know! I know! — wait and you will get me, too. But
not yet to-day. (Wiping the perspiration from his mighty
forehead.) Like my father! — one ought to be a beast
like myself! To get provoked perchè people are living and
forgetting. — (A pause looking around gloomily.) Naturally . . .
not even masks! (the pigeons are cooing below the eaves.)
I understand! — Yes! — — — You went to sleep! (As if
surprised looking up the sky.) Oh! Stars?! — (Takes the watch
out of his pocket.) Half past seven — Oh! oh! (Turning he
looks at Petka stretching and reposing in the violet shades of
the dying sunset. One star is quivering as if its spark were
swayed by the wind. There below Marenica the electric lights
are piercing the green twilight of Lapad with little golden needles
and are scattering into the dead bay.) Petka! — — — well —
if they are all sleeping you almeno[2] are always keeping
awake! (Half aloud) Silly! — you are more beautiful then in
my youth! — — — And for whom? Who is looking at
you? To' whom do you mean anything? — — — (Returning
wearily towards the house.) Here you are! — — — I turned
my back upon you! (Sinks down into the chair absorbed in
his thoughts.) — Petka has been looking so much on this
terrace may be' that accounts fro her gloominess, for
pretty soon nobody will be upon it! Well, soon an
American will come along people will tell him that evil
spirits have been walking upon it. (With a bitter smile.) Ha! —
ha! — They won't have lied! And he will throw the house
and the terrace like Lorko! (He rises, old, rigid, slow.) But
what is the matter with me to-day?! — — — I have no
peace! — — — In vain! — there is nothing more for me
neither walk — nor world — nor anything! — — —
I shall have to stay at home — lock myself up — not

---

[1] Well said.
[2] At least.

see anybody! — — — so they won't· say I have grown foolish ... Yes! — Yes! (following the deep, deafening roar of his thoughts.) Niko, Mare and I! — And Finis! Every morning when we look at each other I feel like saysing: "What?! — You are still here!" (Looking all around.) Alone! — alone! — A thousand years of blood — brains — of real life. And now — here! ... four bones under the cypresses. (Gazing like Niko at the font) "Dead waters" — as the late Orsat used to say. Just so! (Shrugging scornfully his shoulders.) And I am talking like a chatterbox. It is well, poor Mare did not hear me. — She would tell me to drink orange tea for my nerves .... ha! ha! Altrochè nervi![1] — — — (He wants to go into the room.)

Vuko (coming from the garden like a gigantic sentinel has kept his slender figure in the quiet strenght of his most beautiful body, simply):
Master! — — —

Master Luksha (stopping and half turning around):
Who are you?

Vuko (as above):
Vuko from Konavlje.

Master Luksha (coming lazily, ill-humoured to the little table):
Ah! it is you.

Vuko: I put away the casks and shut up the store-house.

Master Luksha: And the keys?

Vuko (handing them over to him):
Here they are! — and you know, master! I watered your horses — and then I go away before dawn!

Master Luksha (putting away the keys into the little table): ·
Did you have your supper?

Vuko (smiling, his teeth shining white under his dark moustache):
I should say! like a beg! Beans and a piece of dry bread!

---

[1] How not for nerves.

Master Luksha (involuntarily):
> Nothing less! (Thoughtful.) Lest I forget, when are you coming back?

Vuko: To-morrow we pick grapes in Bjelina near Ljuta. There will be work for two days! —

Master Luksha (going toward the house):
> Ben![1] — and now adio! — Put out the light in the stables before you fall asleep! — — —

Vuko: Right you are, master; a candle and my sleep! — — —

Master Luksha (stops looking at him. The cold light of the starry sky is reflecting upon the firm forehead of the young man):
> And you sleep well, do you!?

Vuko (passing his hand over the back of his head and looking at his palm he laughs):
> Well it depends! — — — All day long we toil, dig, roll stones our Lord forgive, — like beasts! and at night, gracious me, I throw myself down and fall asleep like dead!

Master Luksha (as above):
> That's why you are such men!

Vuko (spitting on the ground):
> But there are days, master, when something is choking me. Not an eye closed, not a wink of sleep — but everything whirling around and stifling me, God help me, a mere nightmare.

Master Luksha (laughing he wants to go again):
> I know, — know it! — — — (waving his hand) and now I hope you will fall asleep!

Vuko (without moving, passing his handkerchief over his face, gazing fixedly and sighing):
> Ah! if the Lord and the blessed Virgin would — but . . . . .

Master Luksha (at the door, surprised, frowning but inquisitive):
> But — — — what?

---

[1] Well.

V u k o (looking at the east, his fingers getting entangled and crackling like dry branches in the fire):
How shall I fall asleep, Master, when they don't give me Jela?!

M a s t e r L u k s h a (crossing his hands behind his back he comes nearer looking mockingly into his face):
Ah — ma bravo! Let me see you!

V u k o (bowing his head and turning his white sleeves): .
Well! so it is, master! — ever since our parents sent us out to pasture! She was a little child, like a lamb. And how I watched over her! It was for her I picked strawberries and narcissuses. For her! — What do you want? ... A boy .... like a boy!

M a s t e r L u k s h a (as above):
And now when we are grown up we come to our Master under pretence of new wine, — and steal his girls!

V u k o (looking quietly at him):
It isn't so, master, I beg her of you, and it is your will whether you want to give her to me or not.

M a s t e r L u k s h a (turning his back on him):
And I won't give her to you. — Now you will be able to fall asleep!

V u k o (motionless):
And why don't you give her to me?

M a s t e r L u k s h a (swiftly, eye to eye):
And who taught you to ask: Why?

V u k o (passing his hand over his face he gazes steadily into the distance):
Life is very hard for me, master! ....

M a s t e r L u k s h a (looking sideways at him, calmly):
It might be! (Almost mockingly.) He has nothing, the ·big child, and wants to marry!

V u k o (as above):
I have two hands.

Master Luksha (ill-humoured):
You might have four! — No and no! — And her mother was begging me: don't let her, master, marry nobody — yes — yes — she just said: nobody! —

Vuko (putting his hands to his sides. He looks up where the stars are quivering):
And whose fault is it?

Master Luksha: Fault? — I don't understand you.

Vuko (looking down upon the ground, quietly:
Ah! You don't know that, master. She meant to say: my daughter is not for a — bastard.

Master Luksha (coming slowly towards him and looking into his face):
And you are? — — —

Vuko (as above):
They brought me in my swaddling cloth from the hospital. (A pause.)

Master Luksha (turning around lost in thoughts and somewhat out of tune):
I am sorry for you. I believe you are honest, you are surely better than many of our people, oh! — do not doubt! But squeeze your soul and find another girl.

Vuko (passing both hands over his face as if washing. He sighs deeply turning slowly around to go):
What can I do! — When you don't want to — — —

Master Luksha (stiffly towards the room):
E tanto basta![1] — — — look out you are early — — —

Vuko (taking a letter out of his belt):
This here from the priest of Chilip.

Master Luksha (taking the letter and looking at Vuko):
From Dum Ivan? — — — And you are giving it to me now?! ...

[1] And so much enough.

V u k o (calmly):

,He told me to give it to you if you don't let me . . .

M a s t e r   L u k s h a (angrily putting the letter into his pocket):

Ah! — You may tell him right now I sent him my regards and that his trouble is in vain. — — — Ma sapete![1] . . . (Going towards the background. Twilight has covered the entire terrace as with ashes. Only the sky is bright and high, high.)

M a d a m   M a r e (appearing at the door of the room holding a lighted double candle stick. She calls calmly):

— Luksha! . . .

V u k o (close to the exit of the garden, deeply sadly bending his head, he is digging with his finger into the cold stone):

Alas! — How miserable I am, my Lord! . . .

M a d a m   M a r e (startles, still holding the candle she steps toward the voice, horror flitting across her face):

What did you say! — — — Luksha . . . For heaven's sake what is the matter with you!

M a s t e r   L u k s h a (turning around he remains as if rooted to the spot watching how Mare like an apparition approaches Vuko. Involuntarily in a low tone to himself):

Mare! — ┬ —

V u k o (waving his hands he wipes off a tear with the end of his sleeve, then turns around as if to descend; in a low, plaintive voice like drawling out a mountain song):

Alas! How hard it is to be alone! (Descends and goes away.)

M a d a m   M a r e (as above):

Tell me, — tell me, Luksha mine! Your troubles — as then —

M a s t e r   L u k s h a (his face quite transfigured approaches her. The fire of his eyes pierces her empty pupils with an unutterable look out of which a terrible thought is growing louder, but like a breath):

Mare! . . .

M a d a m   M a r e (has felt his breath, moving forward she catches his outstretched hands. The candle trembles in her hand. With an exclamation):

---

[1] But you know.

Ah! here you are! — oh! Why don't you speak to me? ...
I am your only sister! — — — Ah! only don't speak in
that voice. — Then you said too, the same words: How
hard it is — — — Oh! how is that — — —

Master Luksha (as above. All his life is centered in the glance,
with which he is drinking in those pale lips, those empty eyes,
with the longing of a man who wants to find out what the face
of destiny looks like. In a deep voice, close to her joining on to
her words):
How hard it is to be alone (taking slowly the candlestick out of
her hand, he places it upon the little table).

Madam Mare (pressing close to him):
Yes! — Yes! It is the first time to-day you are talking to
me with the voice of your youth, — — — Oh! — How
you felt it! (Caressing him.) My poor Luksha! — — — You,
too, obeyed our fathers! — You left her! — — — You
see — even to-day I remember your weeping — — — Oh!
What is the matter with you — — — What is the matter?

Master Luksha (slowly going away from her his face darkens like
Minchetta in the rain. Automatically, looking incessantly at the
apparition of Mare, he takes out a letter from his pocket, the one
Vuko brought him and opens it trembling convulsively. To himself with immense amazement):
My voice — — — in him? (quickly bending towards the light
he flies over the letter. It is an instant. His face is veiled like in
smoke. His hand relaxes, but he remains firm like speechless
marble. His eyes are staring into the dark, his lips whispering
involuntarily, hardly audible): Vuko! — — — my son! — — —

Madam Mare (agitated, alone, like lost):
Where are you? — — — where? — — —

Master Luksha (closes his eyes as if an overstrong light was scorch-
ing him. The fatal moment has past, it left him crushed. At last
her voice wakes him. He passes a hand over his face like brushing
away a kind of mist. Reviving his first glance falls upon the
miserable woman. He feels like crying, but Luksha Menze to weep
before his sister! Coming close upon her he grasps Madam Mare
as if to embrace her and kissing her white cheeks controlling
himself he bursts out into careless laughter):
Ha! Ha! Ha! — — — I caught you — — — I caught you!

Madam Mare (joyfully though not believing she embraces him, tears streaming from her dead eyes):
Ah! You are yourself again! — But what is it — — — What?

Master Luksha (as above):
You know voices — yes — but yet you are not a real witch. Oh! No! — for you did not guess whether it was weeping or singing you heard — — —

Madam Mare (unbelieving):
Ah! — whether it was singing?!

Master Luksha (more and more animated, the old struggle being fought upon his tortured face):
Certainly! — Look here my old days when I used to make poetry have returned to me! That foolish Dum Marin asked me to compose something for the feast of Saint Michael! — — — That's it! — — — I was reciting and you got scared!

Madam Mare (resting her head upon his shoulder):
Oh! If you knew how I shivered, when I heard you sobbing thus. I don't have anybody but you, — and it is dark !....

Master Luksha (slowly taking her to the room):
It comes all from your not obeying me! — Vica must lead you, or you must call me. And now go — go into your chamber; have supper ready soon, — and I shall read to you the poem I made up to-day ....

Madam Mare (reaching the door she caresses his face with both her hands):
I am going! I am going! — — — Gracious me! Now you have again the voice of your old age! (Kissing him on his forehead) Forgive — in place of our mother! (going away slowly, smiling blissfully.)

Master Luksha (alone he stops at the door looking at her, then turns lazy, grown old, crushed he totters up to a chair. Sinking into it and for a minute gazes at the open letter, then takes it up shaking his head, trembling, defeated, he reads):
"Have pity on the child his mother brought from the hospital 24 years ago. She was called Nika, and was a servant girl in your mother's house. She died immediately from suffering

and shame. On her death bed she told me: When he gets
into misery let his father help him. God is calling me! He
knows I bore him with Master Luksha." (The letter drops
out of his hand and he fixes his gaze into distance.) And she
told the truth. (A pause. He rises, his legs as heavy as lead.)
How everything comes back and how everything gets paid
for! (Harder.) One must pay! (Thoughtfully looking at a ray
in the darkness enfolding him.) A little branch upon an old
tree! — — — And Mare recognized him! Yes — yes — it
is he — he, whom my fathers forbade to come to life —
my son! — — — (In a low tone looking around frightened.) I
have a son!.... In him is all our noble blood! My poor
nono[1]! Oh! If anybody should hear me! (Still more low.)
Everything like our forefathers. (Stepping forward he fixes
his eyes upon emptiness.) Galatea, too, revived, but the soul?
(Night has covered everything. Everywhere stars upon the sky
and upon the sea. Entire nature is melting into darkness and
into sacred stillness. He shivers as if he were cold.) And will
the soul? — (Hard.) It must. (Going heavily and wearily to the
parapet he calls out into the night): Vuko!

The voice of Vuko (from below):
Master!

Master Luksha (as above):
Come up.

The voice of Vuko (as above):
Here I am! —

Master Luksha (coming thoughtfully towards the chapel, involuntarily gazing at the closed doors).

Vuko (appearing at the garden gate. The candles on the little table
are lighting him up. Calmly):
What is your command, Master!

Master Luksha (walking without looking at him):
I wanted to tell you I read the letter of your priest. (As
if looking for it on the little table.) Did he tell you what he
wrote to me?

[1] Grandfather.

Vuko: He did not.

Master Luksha (taking the candle with one hand, the letter with the other one):
Well, come here! (Vuko comes up to him. Luksha hands him the letter looking at him, greedily in a strained way, severely while all the light falls upon the man from Konavlje.) Do you know how to read?

Vuko (with a quiet smile):
How should I — a laborer?

Master Luksha (looking incessantly at him and putting the candle upon the little table):
Whose are you?

Vuko (as above):
And how does this concern you, master!

Master Luksha (lowering his gaze upon the little table he sits down in the chair offering him another one):
Sit down.

Vuko (sits down quietly, according to peasant fashion resting his arms upon his knees).

Master Luksha (naturally without moving his eyes from him):
Your priest tells me he knew your mother — — —

Vuko (as above, looking down upon the ground):
So I heard.

Master Luksha (as above):
That she died while you were in your swaddling cloth — and that she begged him to find your father.

Vuko (indifferently shrugging his shoulders):
What should I want him for, now!

Master Luksha (struggling with his own suffering, a little deeper):
Did you seek him?

Vuko (watching the palm of his hand):
Why should I! — — — I grew up in Mato Milosh' house like his own child. At first the children used to mock me:

"spurious child — — — bastard!" Sometimes it hurt me — but when I saw there were some of them in each house, of Konavlje, I thought: well — it probably must be so!

Master Luksha (as above):
And later on — you suffered! Ah!?

Vuko (seated comfortably in his chair):
No, I did not. First to pasture — eh! those were my most beautiful years, — and then toil, cut, dig .... In summer in the heat, in winter on the water. Well! here you have it, master!

Master Luksha (looking more piercingly at him):
And did never anything torture you, stifle you to get out of this poverty, — to be something — — — a "gentleman"?

Vuko (taking out his handkerchief and blowing his nose smiling naively):
To tell you right, I should have gone to America.

Master Luksha (glowering):
And why? —
Vuko (frankly):
To earn money!

Master Luksha (as above):
What do you want money for?

Vuko (rising, putting his hands on his hips — laughing):
Well, master! I should have come back to Konavlje to buy some land of my master.

Master Luksha (with a last ray of hope):
And the children? ....

Vuko (ashamed, scratching behind his ears):
Children! — — — Goodness me! — — — who is thinking of that .... (Deeply.) Especially since — you won't give her to me!

Master Luksha (slowly going to the chapel he returns lost in thoughts):
And what would you say if somebody should suddenly

tell you: You know, Vuko! — —.— Your father was a nobleman — — — He died and on his deathbed he left money to you — and a house — a big one let's say per esempio[1] (close to him, pale but struggling as for his own salvation, watching his beautiful brave forehead) — such one like mine! —.— —

Vuko (laughing between his thick moustaches):
Alas, master! What are you mocking me!

Master Luksha (as above):
I am speaking the way people talk. I cannot go to sleep. It does not make any difference to me with whom I am talking! — — — Dunque (putting his hands on his heroic shoulders) answer me: if the doors of this house opened to you, the servants saluted and received you, and somebody stretched out his hands saying to you: This is the palace of your fathers, you are a nobleman!..... Well, well, it won't do to feel ashamed! — It is a joke. — — — But there were similar tales in life. Dunque! What would you do, Vuko, if they gave you this house? — — — —

Vuko (laughing lively and showing all his teeth):
Well! — to tell you right, master (looking all around) — I should sell it.

Master Luksha (as if something has struck his breast, he sits down in his chair starting to laugh convulsively):
Sell! — ha! ha!

Vuko (as above, calmly, spitting on the ground):
And how! — and I should go to Konavlje to plant the wine.

Master Luksha (silenced he bends his head. The sentence has been pronounced. Taking Dum Ivan's letter, he tears it slowly. To himself):
So it is! (Simply to Vuko with an expression of his former superiority He rises.) You will tell Master Dum Ivan you saw me tearing up his letter.

---

[1] For example.

Vuko (going away towards the gate):
I will, master!

Master Luksha (watching him):
Where are you going?

Vuko: Into the stable.

Master Luksha (blinking his eyes, he lowers his gaze and after
a moment's hesitation quietly):
Well, go!

Vuko (wanting to descend):
Good night, master!

Master Luksha (writing quickly something upon the paper, he hands
it to him):
And this you will deliver to Dum Ivan.

Vuko (takes it looking at him with eyes full of desire and prayer):
Master! — — —

Master Luksha (gazing at his face, almost to himself):
You forgot your soul, Pigmalion! . . . .

Vuko (as above):
What are you saying, Master?

Master Luksha (calmly):
Nothing. That you will marry Jela in a fortnight —

Vuko (lively, quickly, beaming he bends and kisses his hands):
My master!

Master Luksha (placing his hand into his, he stops gazing
steadily into his beautiful face. Whispering as to himself):
What a shame! (He shakes himself, straightens up and goes
away toward the house.) — And you will go to America and
intanto[1] — go to bed.

Vuko (going away merrily):
Oh! — How could I now, master! —

[1] Meanwhile.

Master Luksha (listening to his vanishing steps. A subdued song of Vuko's happiness is heard. Then he sighs deeply and peace descends upon his face):

If Dum Marin could have heard me — — — and what about theories! — — — (Taking the candle he calls Vica from the terrace): Vica!

Master Luksha (as above):

When Vuko leaves, — close the door!...

The voice of Vica: I will, master!

Master Luksha (gowing towards the room but stopping, the candle in his hand, he drinks in with one deep glance all the black darkness of the dead dusky terrace. He seems to be above the tombstones of some old cemetery. Shivering, he makes a sign with his hand as if driving away invisible ghosts. More stooping, older, he goes into the room):

And now! — Let's go to bed! (He enters.)

(C u r t a i n.)

**THIS BOOK IS DUE ON THE LAST DATE
STAMPED BELOW**

AN INITIAL FINE OF 25 CENTS

WILL BE ASSESSED FOR FAILURE TO RETURN
THIS BOOK ON THE DATE DUE. THE PENALTY
WILL INCREASE TO 50 CENTS ON THE FOURTH
DAY AND TO $1.00 ON THE SEVENTH DAY
OVERDUE.

APR 17 1939

JAN 26 1942

FEB 13 1936

9 Dec'53 B M

RET'D APR 17 1984

3 Apr'56 P W

APR 9 1956

SENT ON ILL

MAR 1 2 2007

30 Mar'58 M H

U.C. BERKELEY

IN STACKS
JUL 3 0 1969 75

JUL 1 6 '69

AUG 3 0 1969

IN STACKS

JUN 2 6 '69

SEP 3 0 1969

LD 21—95m-7,'37

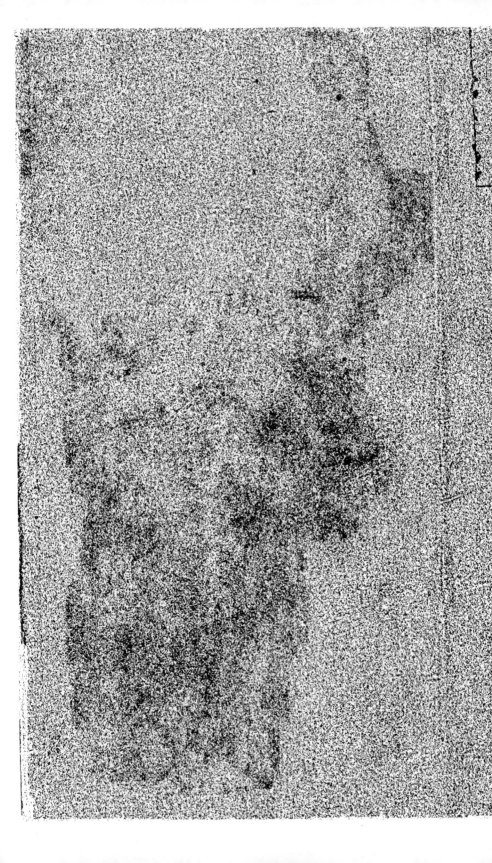

Lightning Source UK Ltd.
Milton Keynes UK
UKHW02f1820151018
330597UK00030B/1440/P